ZOMBIE WATERS

A RICK WATERS NOVEL

CARIBBEAN ADVENTURE SERIES
BOOK SIXTEEN

ERIC CHANCE STONE

LOST AND FOUND
PUBLISHING

ZOMBIE WATERS

Eric Chance Stone

CHAPTER

ONE

Rick and the team landed in New Orleans after making a few connections in Egypt. The flight arrived in the morning, but they were all hungry, so Rick suggested a restaurant where he had eaten several times before. He grew up in Beaumont, Texas, and with New Orleans being just under four hours away, Rick visited frequently.

Criollo Restaurant was on the corner of Royal and Iberville Street in the heart of the French Quarter. It was located in the Hotel Monteleone and had been a staple for locals and tourists alike since 2012. Rick had stumbled upon it by accident while working on a case in New Orleans a few years prior.

The entire team was present, with the exception of Clay, Gary's private pilot; Johnie, who worked on Rick's yacht as first mate and master diesel mechanic; and Pee-Roy, captain of Gary's expedition treasure-hunting ship.

Jules, Rick's fiancée, secured a table for them. Rick sat beside her next to Gary and Possum. Gary and Possum had gone to school with Rick back in Fannett, TX, a small rice field community not far from Beaumont. When people asked Rick where he was from, he usually said Beaumont, even though he grew up in Fannett. No one had ever heard of Fannett.

"Who wants beignets?" asked Rick.

They all nodded as the waiter poured fresh Community brand coffee into their cups. Rick was beyond happy. He loved Community Coffee. Community originated in Baton Rouge, Louisiana, but had a strong presence in Texas, where Rick grew up.

"Ahhh, I've missed that," said Rick.

After spending more time in Egypt than he had wanted working on a case, he was glad to be back in a more traditional setting that fit his roots. Rick ordered a round of beignets for the table and cracked open the menu.

"What's good here, Rick?" asked Gary.

Gary joined Rick's private investigation firm a few years ago after reconnecting at The Boudin Hut, an infamous juke joint in Port Arthur, Texas. Rick bought Gary a few drinks and dinner, and they caught up on old times. A few weeks later, Gary won one of the largest Powerball drawings in U.S. history. He invested in Rick's business and became a full partner shortly after.

"You know, to be honest, I've never eaten breakfast here. I can tell you about several items from the dinner menu, and I have never had a bad meal here. I heard the breakfasts are amazing, so that's why I picked the place. I'm sure anything you get will be incredible," replied Rick.

"Anyone want to try smoked bacon?" asked Possum.

They all nodded, so Rick told the waiter to bring enough for everyone when the meals arrived. Possum's real name was Thomas Michael Jackson. Yes, Michael Jackson. He loved to listen to George Jones, whose nickname was "The Possum." Somewhere down the line, and no one remembers exactly who—although Rick takes credit for it—someone started calling Mike "Possum" and it stuck.

In addition to being involved in a missing person case in Cairo, Egypt, Possum devised a ruse to gain access to the lower caves and corridors of the Pyramid of Khafre. The ruse was that they were filming a prequel to "Raiders of the Lost Ark" called "Indiana Jones and the First Astronaut." Possum wanted to investigate the conspiracy theory that there was an ancient alien power plant beneath the pyramid which descended two kilometers and he got more than he bargained for. He discovered that the columns beneath the pyramids were part of an Iranian uranium enrichment reactor. This led to the discovery of an underground lab and city that was connected by tunnels to other cities via a high-speed Maglev train system. It was all secret, hidden from the public, and funded by the WEF. Possum and the crew managed to melt down the reactor, stopping a potential war with Iran that the military-industrial complex always wanted, and destroyed the tunnel system to over twelve underground cities throughout Europe and North Africa.

"I think I'm going to have Lobster Benedict," said Jules.

"That sounds good, baby. I might get the Cajun omelet," said Rick.

Everyone ordered and they discussed the upcoming film shoot. While using a fake film as a ruse in Egypt, Possum discovered he had quite a knack as a director and filmmaker. A Hollywood makeup artist named Richard had flown out to Egypt to assist with Gary's transformation into Dr. Henry Jones. Richard had talked Gary into investing in a film he was working on in New Orleans called *Bayou of the Dead*, a modern take on a classic zombie horror flick. Gary had agreed to invest in the film on the one condition that he and Rick get to be zombie extras in the movie. Richard was so impressed with Possum's debut directorial skills that once the director on his film quit because the production crew was on a SAG strike, he asked Possum if he would step in and finish the film and use the German production company he had used in Egypt, since they were not a part of SAG. Even though they were non-union, Gary agreed to pay all their expenses and pay them union scale. The assistant director, Paul, was flying in later that day, ahead of the rest of the crew, to scout locations.

The film in Egypt came out so well that Possum decided to finish it and use the mobile AVID editing trailer that was on location for the zombie film during breaks while shooting. He planned to find a Hollywood distributor and do a limited theatrical release. No one, not even Rick, knew Possum intended to do that. They all assumed he might finish it and burn it to DVD to watch as a spoof one night over laughs and drinks, affectionately known by the gang as ha-ha, clink-clink.

"Good news y'all. I just got a text from Johnie. He has had enough of his vacation in Fort Myers, and he's driving my motorhome to New Orleans. We can use it to chill out between takes on the set. He also hired another guy to drive your bus here, Gary," said Rick.

"Sweet! I miss my Prevost."

"Yay, Johnie! Oh, that means Chief is coming with him, right?" asked Jules.

"You're damn straight!" exclaimed Rick.

Chief was Rick's umbrella cockatoo and had become a part of the family. Jules loved Chief, and they were extremely close. It was amazing how affectionate a cockatoo could be.

"Where are we staying?" asked Possum.

"Well, I was thinking about that. A lot of filming will be over at the Bayou Sauvage National Wildlife Refuge. That's east of here, about twenty-five minutes. There aren't any five-star hotels out that way. We need to decide whether we want to be closer to the set and stay in a lower-star hotel with nothing to do on breaks or stay here in New Orleans and make the commute. I personally think we should stay here in New Orleans, especially since the motorhome and bus will be on set. What do y'all think?" asked Rick.

"I think we should stay at the Windsor Court," said Jules with a sly grin.

Gary picked up his iPhone and looked it up. It was a five-star hotel just off Canal Street in downtown New Orleans, not far from the French Quarter.

"Great choice, Jules. I second that idea. So does everyone say aye?"

They all agreed, so Gary booked rooms for everyone. He

would arrange accommodations for the German production company closer to the set, as they usually had to arrive first on shooting days. After breakfast, they all wanted to stroll around the French Quarter a bit, taking in the sights and walking off their meal. Gary, being Gary, was ready for a beer, and it was only 10:15 a.m., so they stopped at Lafitte's Blacksmith Shop, known not only as the oldest bar in New Orleans but also believed by many to be the oldest bar in the United States, dating back to 1722.

"Do y'all have Busch Light?" asked Gary.

"We sure do," replied the bartender.

A moment later, he came back to the bar with a Busch Light tallboy and a tray with four purple-colored shots on it.

"What are these?" asked Gary.

"Purple Dranks. The first round is on me. Trust me, you'll like it." Gary took the two meant for Rick and Jules since they didn't drink alcohol anymore and passed one to Possum. Possum pushed it back to Gary. It was too early for him to drink. Gary downed all four shots and took a big swig from his Busch Light.

The bartender shook his head as he watched Gary.

"You probably shouldn't have done that."

"Why, what's in them?"

"Two parts bourbon, one part Everclear, and one part grape juice, shaken over ice."

"Everclear?"

"Yep," said the bartender.

"Oops," replied Gary.

"Let's head to the hotel," said Rick.

Jules ordered an XL Uber, and they hung out on Bourbon Street, people-watching until it arrived. By the time they reached the hotel, Gary was slurring a little. After they checked in, Rick and Jules had to help Gary to his room. He insisted he was fine as he staggered into his room, dragging his suitcase on its side, with the wheels not touching the floor. Jules snickered as the door shut behind him. They walked down the hall to their room.

"Rick, they have a spa. Wanna do a couples massage?" asked Jules.

"Hell yeah! Let me call them real quick."

Rick dialed the number and learned there was an opening in fifteen minutes. He held his hand over the phone and asked Jules if she could be ready that quickly. She gave him a thumbs up and unpacked both of their bags, placing the clothes in the dresser. Rick loved that about her. She always fully unpacked their luggage and organized it in dressers, even if they were just staying overnight some-where. She said she hated living out of a suitcase and that by putting the clothes away and her bathroom items where they belonged, it always made her feel at home, no matter where she was. Rick had grown accustomed to her pampering him. Rick confirmed their massage and changed into shorts and a tank top. Jules put on shorts and a halter top as well. They were about to head out when Rick's phone buzzed.

Hey Rick, I'm heading to the rooftop pool if you need me.

No worries, Possum. We're going to do a couples massage. We'll probably check it out after.

10-4

The masseuses were both female. The Creole women wore red bandanas. That look always made Rick think of Marie Laveau, the most famous Voodoo Queen who hailed from New Orleans. Incense was burning in the corner of the room, and soft music played in the background.

"Ça va?" asked the woman as she poured warm oil over her hands.

"I'm good. Don't worry about being gentle. I like a deep, hard massage," said Rick.

Rick was fluent in Cajun Creole, and it made her comfortable.

"D'où vous venez?"

"I'm originally from Beaumont, but we live in Florida. Jules is from Colombia."

Creole was a mix of French, English, and Jamaican Patois. Rick understood most of it but wasn't fluent in the French part every time.

The woman massaging Jules didn't speak much and got right down to business. She was moaning and groaning every time the woman used too much pressure. Rick tried not to laugh but she heard him.

"Shut up, Rick Waters. It hurts."

"Hurts so good," sang Rick, trying to emulate John Cougar.

After the massage, they were handed some cucumber-infused water.

"Drink plenty, Ami," said Rick's masseuse.

Rick had three glasses. He tipped them well, and they headed back up to their room.

"Wanna hit the pool?" asked Rick.

"They have a pool?"

"Yep, it's on the roof. Possum is there now."

"Sweet, let me grab my suit. Wear those new Hurley board shorts I bought you."

"Okay, Jules. I've been wanting to try them."

If it were up to Rick, he'd wear the same damn shorts he bought at Walmart years ago, but Jules made him throw them out. She always upgraded his attire, and he didn't complain about it. When they got to the pool, the only other person there was Possum. He was lying in a lounge chair with his head buried in a New Orleans book he borrowed from the little library attached to the business center.

"Whatcha reading?" asked Rick.

"Haunted New Orleans: History & Hauntings of the Crescent City."

"Any good?" asked Rick.

"Kinda interesting. It says this hotel is haunted."

"Really?"

"That's what it says. The place where we had breakfast is also haunted. According to this book, there are numerous haunted hotels in the area," said Possum.

"I bet. There is so much history here. I love the architecture of New Orleans. That, plus the cuisine, are my favorite things about the Big Easy."

"Yeah, the food here is amazing."

"Have you seen Gary?"

"Nope. I texted him a couple of times but got no response," said Possum.

"Think I should check on him?" asked Rick.

"Couldn't hurt."

"Okay, I'll go check on him before I jump in the pool. Be right back. Jules, I'm gonna go check on Gary. Wanna go?"

"Nah, go ahead. I wanna get some sun before it disappears."

Rick took the stairs down to their floor and knocked on the door of Gary's room. There was no answer. He knocked several times.

"Gary, you in there?" asked Rick as he knocked.

He put his ear to the door and didn't hear anything. A housekeeper came around the corner pushing a cart, and Rick got her attention.

"Excuse me, I left my key in the room. Can you let me inside? My wallet is in there, too, if you need it."

It was a little white lie, but Rick didn't want to go all the way down to the front desk to get the manager to open up Gary's room.

She opened the door for Rick and went back to pushing her cart, uninterested in seeing his ID.

"Thank you."

The woman nodded. As Rick stepped into the room, there was Gary, passed out face-first on the couch, still in his clothes. Rick made sure he was breathing but let him sleep. He took one of the extra keys to Gary's room and headed back to the pool.

"Find Gary?" asked Possum.

"Yep, he's passed out on the couch."

Jules started laughing.

"Dang Purple Dranks!" she exclaimed.

Rick settled into a lounge chair beside Jules and looked

up at the big TV hanging behind Possum. There was some talking head on MSNBC discussing an investigation into the possible deportation of an undocumented immigrant who had been spewing anti-American, pro-Hamas propaganda. Rick thought about it and said,

"Calling an illegal alien an undocumented immigrant is like calling a meth dealer an undocumented pharmacist. The issue is not immigration, but rather the illegal aspect."

"Good one, Rick," said Possum without looking up from his book.

Rick took off his tank top and slid into the pool.

"Whoa, it's saltwater. Cool!" said Rick.

"Good. It won't fade your new board shorts. You like 'em?" asked Jules.

"Yep, they fit perfectly. I'm glad they are stretchy, too, because the Cajun food might make them get a little tight. Ha-ha."

"No, Mister! You said we were getting new bikes when we got back from Egypt. I looked on my phone and there is a Trek bicycle shop over in Elmwood. Can we go in the morning?" asked Jules.

"So, you've made your mind up on Trek?"

"I'm pretty sure. I wanna try one. They have the FX Sport SL 4 in stock. It's a fitness bike. They also have the Verve 3 Disc Gen 4, the comfort bike you tried that time."

"Cool, yeah, I like to be a little more upright when I ride. Yeah, we can check 'em out tomorrow. I'll need to rent a car. I'll get us an SUV from the front desk," said Rick.

"They are having a sale on your model and also on that Kuat hitch rack you wanted."

"Sounds like a plan, Jules," said Rick.

Jules jumped out of her lounge chair and did a cannonball into the pool. She was excited to get a new bicycle, especially a carbon fiber Trek. She wanted to get more exercise and get Rick moving more. She swam up to Rick and wrapped her legs around his waist.

"Thank you for agreeing to get me a new bike."

"My pleasure, Jules. You deserve it. Just don't make me ride too much. My butt will hurt."

"We can start slow and work up to more miles. Plus, you've never had a really good bike. I think once you get it, you will want to ride more. Those Trek Verve bikes are super comfortable to ride."

"I'm sure you're right, Jules."

"I'm always right," said Jules as she kissed him and started doing calisthenics in the water.

That's where Rick drew the line, though. Jules used to try to get him to exercise in the pool but gave up trying. Rick always said pools are for chilling out in. Gyms are for working out, and all he ever wanted to do in a pool was bob around and hang from the edge. He loved relaxing in pools and would never exercise in one. Jules conceded as long as he got his exercise elsewhere.

"Where do you wanna eat dinner, Rick?" asked Possum.

"Well, I chose the breakfast spot. You choose."

"Have you ever eaten at Arnaud's?" asked Possum.

"No, but I heard they have amazing duck there. It's Cajun, right?"

"Absolutely! Sound good to you, Jules?"

Jules nodded as she continued to move her legs back and

forth under the water. After relaxing for another hour, Rick and Jules headed back to their room. Possum wanted to finish the chapter he was reading. They planned to have an early dinner, so Rick made reservations for 6:30 p.m. As they walked down the hall, Rick stopped and looked over at Jules.

"Wanna see something funny?" asked Rick.

Jules nodded as Rick used Gary's room key and stepped inside his room. Gary hadn't moved one inch from the position Rick saw him in two hours ago. Jules covered her mouth and laughed.

"We need to get him up. He will miss dinner if we don't," said Rick.

Rick walked over to the couch and gently nudged Gary.

"Hey buddy, wake up. It's almost five o'clock. Gary. Wake up."

Gary yawned, then put his hand on his head.

"Stop yelling. I'm up. I'm up."

"I'm not yelling, buddy. I'm whispering," said Rick.

"Oh, my head! Those damn Purple Dranks! Never again."

"Jules, do you have any Cherry BC Powders in your purse?"

"I think so."

Jules dug around in her purse and finally found two of them. Rick grabbed a bottle of water from Gary's wet bar and opened up both of the BC Powders.

"Here ya go. Try these."

"Thanks, man. Phew. It took me a minute to realize where I was. What time is it?"

"I just told you. It's almost five o'clock."

"Shit! I've been asleep for over four hours," said Gary.

"More like passed out. Listen, we are having dinner at Arnaud's at 6:30 p.m. Can you be ready by then?"

"Oh yeah. I love that place."

"You've been there?"

"Yep. They have great duck."

"So, I've heard. Okay, Jules and I are gonna go shower. We'll meet you in the lobby around six, okay?"

"I'll be there."

Rick showered after Jules and wanted to fool around, but by the time he finished, it was time to get dressed for the restaurant. He'd have to settle for a rain check. They texted Possum to meet them in the lobby and he replied that he was already there with Gary.

When Jules and Rick got to the lobby, Gary was sitting in a plush Victorian-style chair, sipping on a Busch Light tallboy.

"You're incorrigible," said Rick.

"Hair of the dog. I feel like shit. No more Purple Dranks for me."

"That's good to hear. Hair of the dog, I've been there. Don't miss it."

"I know Rick. When you said you were taking a break from drinking, I never dreamed you would quit forever. That's commendable."

"It worked for me. I never planned on being a teetotaler, but I feel good. To each his own. I don't judge anyone."

"I know, Rick. You're a good man. That's why we are friends. Let's eat."

They piled into an Uber XL bound for Arnaud's. The duck was as good as everyone said it was. The meal was wonderful, and they were all feeling jet lagged, so they called it an early night. When they returned to the hotel, Rick arranged through the front desk to rent an SUV and have it delivered in the morning. They all went to their rooms for the night. Everyone was asleep before ten o'clock.

TWO

Rick received a call from the front desk informing him that he needed to come down to the lobby to sign for his car rental. Jules was sipping coffee and told him she would stay in the room. Rick took the elevator down and met the man from Enterprise Rent-A-Car. To his surprise, they had upgraded him to a Jeep Gladiator Mojave. He had always wanted to try one. He loved his Ford Bronco but was considering the Jeep trucks. Rick signed the papers and thanked the man. Normally, he would have to drive the delivery guy back to the Enterprise location, but they had another delivery, and one of his colleagues was sitting outside in a Tesla that needed to be delivered. Rick also thanked the front desk clerk for letting him know the Jeep had arrived and headed back up to his room.

"Jules, they gave us a Gladiator."

"What's that?" she asked.

"You know, one of those new Jeep trucks."

"Oh, cool. Those are cute."

"Cute? More like badass!"

"Maybe badass to you, but cute to me."

"You are so funny, Jules."

"I know, but you love me."

"I do!"

"I do too."

"Maybe we should say 'I do' to a priest or a minister."

"We have been engaged for quite some time. I'm ready when you are, big boy."

"Noted!"

Rick knew it was time to make Jules his wife. They were perfect for each other and always planned to get married. Work seemed to get in the way every time. He wanted it to be special. Neither of them wanted a big wedding; they just wanted it to be unique and memorable. He also wanted to surprise her. He had to put his thinking cap on and figure something out. But for now, it was time for a bagel. They had sesame seed bagels delivered to the room. Rick buttered one up and tossed it in the microwave to warm it. He devoured it.

"Are you ready to do some bike shopping?"

"Early bird eats the worm."

"You mean early bird gets the worm, right?"

"Well, duh, it has to get the worm to eat it," said Jules.

"Okay, never mind."

Rick had grown so accustomed to Jules saying idioms incorrectly that he found it cute.

They took the elevator down to the parking garage and climbed into the Jeep.

"Wow, fancy!" exclaimed Jules.

Rick synced his iPhone to the big screen on the Jeep's dashboard and plugged in the address to Google Maps. The route took them down Hwy 90 right past the Superdome. Jules snapped a few pictures with her phone. The trip only took twenty minutes. They arrived shortly after the place opened.

"Good morning, welcome to Trek. I'm Thomas, how can I help you?"

"We're looking for a couple of bikes. I'm Rick, and this is Jules. She wants to try out the Trek FX 4 carbon fiber bike and I'm more interested in one of those Verve comfort bikes."

"Great, we have two Trek FX 4s in stock; both are white: a medium and an XL. I think the medium would be perfect for your wife."

"Oh, we're not married," said Rick.

"Soon," said Jules playfully.

That sealed it for Rick. He was embarrassed that he had even said that. He should've never corrected the salesman. He just hoped it didn't hurt Jules' feelings deep down.

"And you are in luck. The Verve 3 Disc Gen 4 is on sale."

"I read that online. $749, down from $999, right?"

"Actually, as of this morning, all remaining models are $549."

"No shit?"

"Yep, I got the email from corporate this morning. The prices haven't even been changed online," said Thomas.

"Hook me up, bro."

"I have one large in stock. You could either try a large or an XL. You're right on the bubble."

"I'll try both."

"Good idea. Let me grab y'all a couple of helmets. You can go all the way down Webb Street to Central and back. That'll give you a good idea."

Rick sat on the bike and leaned back.

"Is this as high as the handlebars go back? I like to be as upright as possible."

"Let me adjust the stem back a little."

Thomas grabbed an Allen wrench and moved the stem all the way back, making the handlebars higher.

"That's better. Let's roll, Jules."

Thomas helped them roll the bikes out of the front door, and Rick tightened his helmet as Jules took off like a rocket. Rick tried to catch her, but it was no use. Her bike was as fast as lightning. He slowed down and tried the brakes a few times. The bike was nice; incredibly comfortable. The seat post had a shock absorber in it. It was amazing. He was sold. It felt perfect. There was no need even to try the XL. Jules slowed down, allowing Rick to catch up.

"Oh my God, Rick. This bike is the cat's powwow."

"You mean cat's meow. Never mind. I'm glad you like it."

"I love it!"

"Let's go pay for them," said Rick.

Rick bought the bikes and got a good deal on the Kuat bike rack. Thomas had one built for display and gave it to Rick because he was staying in a hotel, and it required quite a lengthy assembly. Rick loaded the bikes onto the rack he had attached to the Jeep, and they headed back to the hotel. On the way back, he received a text from Possum letting him know Richard and Paul had arrived and they were heading to the Bayou Sauvage National Wildlife Refuge to scout shooting locations.

"Jules, you wanna head over to set? There are some cool spots to ride out there. We may as well get some time on the bikes in."

"Yes, please."

Possum sent Rick a Google Map pin where they would be. Rick typed it in, and they took off. The reserve was east of New Orleans, but not super far from downtown.

"You know they have gators out there, right, Jules?"

"I ain't skeered."

"They also have spiders and snakes."

"Shut up!" exclaimed Jules.

Rick suddenly remembered a song by Jim Stafford and started singing, "I don't like spiders and snakes, and that ain't what it takes to love me, ooh, ooh."

"What are you singing?" asked Jules.

"Hey Siri, play Spiders and Snakes by Jim Stafford," said Rick.

"Playing Spiders and Snakes, by Jim Stafford on Apple Music," said Siri.

Jules listened as Rick sang along to the tune, finding it amusing. They drove through New Orleans, turned onto I-10, and then continued on HWY 20. The closer they got to the refuge, the more it reminded Rick of the bayou where he grew up catching catfish with limb lines, giving him a comforting sense of peace. While many people might feel uneasy around gators and snakes, Rick felt at home. He knew that most gators kept their distance and that cotton-mouth water moccasins wanted nothing to do with humans. In all the years he spent stomping around the bayou and occasionally stepping on a snake basking in the sun on a trail, he never got bitten. That didn't mean he didn't respect them. He, too, kept his distance but never feared them.

"Look, Jules, there's a big one. At least twelve feet long," said Rick as he pointed at a gator basking on the bank in the sun.

Jules quickly grabbed her iPhone and snapped a picture. Rick pulled up beside one of the set trailers. He saw Richard, Paul, and Possum talking a few yards away. He waved at them as he stepped down from the Jeep. Jules stepped out, and they walked over to the guys. Rick and Jules greeted them.

"Nice ride," said Possum.

"Yeah, wait until you see our bikes on the back," replied Rick.

"That's great, y'all. Paul and Richard wanna show us the location of the next shoot. They did a rewrite and decided that a villain was needed in the movie, not just a bunch of zombies trying to eat everyone's brains, but rather a controlled group of zombies created by an evil force. The zombies were brought to life by a spell from a voodoo queen. Jules, you would be perfect to play that part. And Rick, instead of playing a zombie extra, would you be interested in the role of the local sheriff? Both parts have speaking roles," said Possum.

Rick glanced at Jules, and a huge smile spread across her face.

"I'll take that as a yes," said Rick.

"Oh, and we are changing the name of the movie to Voodoo Swamp," added Richard.

"I love it!" exclaimed Jules.

"Just wait and see your wardrobe, Jules. You are going to love it. You will be so beautiful in this film. I mean, you already are, but this will be over the top. A true movie star," said Possum.

Jules was beaming as the reality set in that this was a real film and her face would be on the big screen. She felt anxiety creeping in. Taking a few deep breaths, she tried to think of something else. She remembered she would use the alias Valentina Salsa and had no desire to do any promotions or interviews.

"I ask only one thing. If you want me to be beautiful, can you also make me unrecognizable? Maybe change my nose or eyes or something?"

"Prosthetics take time, Jules, but I can make it happen. I understand you wanting to keep your anonymity, so I got you covered," said Richard.

"Okay, I feel better," replied Jules.

They all walked down a trail through live oaks and Spanish moss. The air was humid and heavy. Sweat clung to their backs as they moved down the narrow path, shoes sinking into soft mud. Vines hung low, and the water on either side was dark and still. The place smelled of rot and wet wood. No one spoke much. A mosquito buzzed close, and Rick slapped at his neck. Trees rose up around them— tall, bare cypress with knees poking through the water like broken stumps. Moss hung from the branches, limp and gray. A bird took off ahead, loud and sudden. They stopped for a moment, watching the ripples where something else had moved in the water. No one said what they were thinking.

The trail turned into a wooden boardwalk in places, old and slick, bending under their weight. Paul paused to take some shots. The rest kept moving, watching their steps, not wanting to slip.

"This'll work," said Paul, the assistant director. He didn't raise his voice. "It's quiet. Feels forgotten."

They walked on, deeper into the bayou. The trees closed in more, and the light dimmed. Suddenly, a loud splash broke the silence. Jules grabbed Rick's arm.

"What was that?" she asked.

"Hard to say. A gator or snapping turtle. No telling."

"Okay, so see that open area over there with the tall grass? We are gonna set up an altar for you to hold a ritual to bring a dead man back to life. That will be a scene to be used earlier in the film, and we will use one of the zombies that we already filmed but put him in his street clothes. He will be zombie number one. Then it will spread. Got it?" Richard explained.

"Got it. Can we trim the grass where the altar will be? I'm not too comfortable walking through that salt grass," said Jules.

"Oh yeah. We will ensure there are no critters and trim the grass. We can shoot the altar with a wide shot before trimming the grass, and then trim it to make sure your ritual is set at least knee high. It won't be an issue," replied Richard.

They scouted out a few more spots to film and returned

to the trailers. Paul grabbed Rick and Jules the new scripts and gave them an extra one for Gary to read. Rick laid the scripts in the Jeep and took the bikes off the rack. Richard unlocked the AVID editing trailer and gave Possum a tour.

"Let's go for a quick ride," said Rick.

Jules climbed onto her bike, and they headed to the Bayou Sauvage Ridge trailhead. According to the map, it was a nine-mile round trip with views of Maxent Lagoon. Thousands of bird species nested in the area. Rick turned on his Merlin Bird ID app and tucked it into his shirt pocket. He also opened his MapMyFitness app and set it for road cycling. Nine miles of walking would be incredibly strenuous and take forever, but on a bicycle, it was an easy first day. The Trek bikes performed better than expected, although Jules had to slow down several times for Rick to catch up. She was more focused on the fitness aspect of the ride, and her bike was designed for that, while Rick enjoyed taking in the sights and listening to the birds. He felt a bit melancholy thinking about Chief and missed him. Soon enough, though, he knew Johnie would arrive in the motorhome, and they would be reunited.

As they made the loop, Rick spotted a couple of guys with shotguns leaning against their pickup. He overtook Jules and stopped next to them. They appeared nervous. He knew they were up to no good but tried to play it off.

"Y'all doing a little hunting?" asked Rick.

"Yeah, that's what we're doing, hunting," said one of the guys with a long, scraggly beard.

The other guy smiled, revealing he was tweaking and had meth mouth.

"Those are some nice bikes," said Meth Mouth.

"Yeah, they are okay," said Rick, trying to downplay their value.

Rick knew meth heads would steal anything of value to sell it for more meth. The last thing he wanted was to lose their bikes on the first day out. He also didn't want a conflict with those losers. It seemed inevitable, though, and they had the guns. He wouldn't put Jules in harm's way, but he damn sure wasn't going to let those losers take his bike. He had to think fast.

Jules could sense the danger and knew from Rick's glance that something was about to go down. Rick wanted her to get out of range of the shotguns if the men bum-rushed them.

"Jules, is your chain still slipping? I can adjust it," said Rick as he stepped off his bike.

He crouched down, pretending to adjust the derailleur. As he did so, he whispered to her to pedal back the way they came. She slid past him and gave it all the gas she had.

"I think that's better. Give it a try," said Rick.

Jules turned her bike around and pedaled a few yards away, then rode back toward Rick and the two meth heads.

"Try it faster, make sure it doesn't slip, then turn around and come back," yelled Rick.

He knew she wouldn't come back, but the two men didn't. As Rick walked back toward his bike the bearded man pumped a shell into his shotgun.

"I think we'll take those bikes," he said.

"Listen, we don't want any trouble. You can have them. Just don't hurt us," replied Rick feigning fear.

He began to push his bike toward the men, keeping one hand on the handlebars and one on the top of the frame.

"Where'd she go?" asked the guy who had pumped his shotgun.

"Here she comes," said Rick as he pointed.

Both men looked to their left, and Rick flung the bike against the gun and into the man's face. He dropped the gun, and Rick picked it up and slammed the stock into his nose. The man went down. Before the other guy could react, Rick swung the gun against his head, knocking him to the ground, then flipped the shotgun around and aimed it at his face.

"Don't fucking move, you scumbag."

The other guy was holding his nose, blood spurting through his fingers.

"Does it hurt?" asked Rick.

The guy looked up, and before he could answer, Rick kicked him in the same place, knocking him out. The other guy on the ground reached for his gun. Rick blasted a hole in the ground a foot away from him. He recoiled like a snake against the truck.

"Stand up!" yelled Rick.

The guy was shaking uncontrollably.

"Empty your pockets...slowly," said Rick.

The guy complied, pulling out a meth pipe and several baggies of dope.

"Don't kill me. Please," begged the man.

"Lift up your friend and put him in the bed of the truck."

Rick had the shotgun inches from his face. The man opened the tailgate and attempted to lift his friend but couldn't manage it alone because he was so frail and meek. Jules arrived back and stood behind Rick.

"Here, keep this on him," Rick said, handing her the shotgun.

She aimed it at the man with a fierce look on her face.

"She's a better shot than me. So, don't try anything," said Rick.

He grabbed the knocked-out guy's arm, and together they shoved him onto the bed of the truck. Rick dug through the pockets and found an even larger bag of meth and another pipe. As Jules kept the shotgun trained on Meth Mouth, Rick opened the cab of the truck and found a roll of nylon string and hooks used for making trotlines. When he opened the glove compartment, he found a pistol with the serial number scratched off and another one under the driver's side seat.

Lovely.

He climbed up into the bed of the truck and hogtied the man using many wraps of nylon string.

"Your turn," said Rick, pointing at the bed of the truck.

The skinny meth head climbed in, and Rick hogtied him as well.

"You boys should thank me. I'm probably saving your lives. You are getting free rehab."

The meth head simply scowled at Rick. He signaled for Jules to pass him the shotgun. He unloaded it, and the shells tumbled into the bed of the truck.

"Well, goodnight," said Rick.

Before the guy could speak, Rick slammed the butt of the gun against his head, knocking him unconscious. Rick then swung the shotgun against the side of the bed, breaking it in half. He jumped down, picked up the other shotgun, unloaded it, and did the same. He tossed that gun into the bed of the truck next to the other one, now in pieces.

"That ought to do it," said Rick.

He pulled out his cell phone and dialed *676 followed by 911.

"911, what is your emergency?"

"There are two meth heads sleeping in the back of their pickup truck near the end of the Bayou Sauvage Ridge trailhead. They have drugs, paraphernalia and several unregistered guns. Can you send an ambulance and a deputy?"

"What is your name, sir?"

"Mudd," said Rick as he hung up.

Rick laughed and climbed back on his bike.

"Dammit!"

"What's wrong?" asked Jules.

"I forgot to pause my MapMyFitness app. Now our time is gonna be screwed up."

CHAPTER
THREE

Rick woke up to pee and felt every muscle in his legs when he stood up. Even though he had only ridden nine miles, he had used muscles he hadn't activated in a while. He made a pot of coffee, turned on the TV to the local news channel, and put it on mute. A few minutes later, Jules awoke, yawned, and went to the bathroom to brush her teeth. Rick took the TV off mute, and shortly after, a reporter appeared on the screen, standing in front of the courthouse and holding a microphone.

"Two Slidell men are currently held in the New Orleans Central Lockup on drug and gun charges. The judge has set their bond at fifty thousand dollars each. An unknown person reported the crime to 911. The sheriff's department reminds local residents to call the police when they see a crime and not to take it into their own hands. The men have been treated for a broken nose, cuts, and contusions. If anyone has any knowledge of the vigilante, they are reminded to call the tips line."

Rick muted the TV again and shook his head.

"Typical, they care more about the criminals than potential victims. Makes me sick," muttered Rick.

He took another sip of his coffee and poured a cup for Jules.

"What's on the agenda today, Mr. Waters?" asked Jules.

"Not sure. Possum said the entire production company from Germany won't be here for a few days, so we're kinda on our own until then, I guess. Wanna take a little trip?"

"To where?"

"I was thinking Nashville. Southwest has four non-stop flights a day, and I have a ton of miles."

"Why Nashville?"

"Remember that time we visited the Opry Mills Hotel?"

"Oh yes, the atrium is so beautiful," replied Jules.

"I was thinking we could get a room there and go down to 2nd Avenue and catch some live country music."

"Sounds amazing! I wanna buy some boots."

"Deal. Why don't you bring the wedding band we bought when we got your engagement ring?" said Rick.

Jules stopped in her tracks, and her eyes welled up.

"Are you saying what I think you're saying?" she asked.

Rick got down on one knee and asked, "Jules Castro, will you marry me?"

"Yes, yes, yes!!!" exclaimed Jules.

"You always said you wanted to get married on a boat. Why don't we get married on that Delta Riverboat that goes around on the river inside the atrium? I think it'd be kind of cool."

"I love that idea," replied Jules.

"I did some research; if we take the 9:30 a.m. flight, we can head straight to the courthouse and get our license. I found a wedding officiant, and she is open tomorrow. She said she has no problem doing it on the riverboat. We need to bring our passports. We could be husband and wife by tomorrow. What do you say?" asked Rick.

"I say yes. One hundred percent yes! I'll pack a bag now."

"Don't bring too much. You can get a white skirt to go with that lace top you have, and I'll buy a nice black shirt and we can wear cowboy hats and make it fun."

"Rick Waters, you are being so romantic. Did you hit your head?"

"Ha-ha. No, I just love you."

"I love you too," said Jules as she threw a bag together.

"What about the guys?"

"There's no time to get your parents here, so I think we should just do this for us, and we can have a celebration later. Sound good?" asked Rick.

"Perfect!"

Rick texted Possum and Gary, informing them that since the production company wasn't in town, they needed a getaway and would be back in a couple of days. Both of them sent thumbs-up back. Possum would be busy editing the movie they shot in Egypt, while Gary would be doing his usual activities. By the time Rick and Jules returned, Johnie, Clay, and Chief would be in New Orleans, where they could tell everyone and throw a big celebration. Instead of returning the Jeep to Enterprise, he called the local location and had them change the daily rental to a weekly. They didn't have time to return it before the flight.

Rick parked in long-term parking, and they checked in. They still had an hour until the flight began boarding, so they stopped at Cafe Du Monde near the Southwest gate and got some beignets and coffee. Jules was so excited about the trip; it was all she could talk about.

"Can we go to the Boot Barn? I want these boots!" said Jules, showing Rick some blue boots with tassels.

"Sure, baby. Whatever you want. Whoa, look at those alligator boots. I'd like to try those on."

After scarfing down a few beignets, they headed to the gate. Despite having booked the tickets only a few hours before they arrived, they got into Group B for boarding. From past experience, Rick knew that anywhere in Group B, they'd be able to sit together on the flight. Once the gate agent called for B1 through B30 to line up, Rick and Jules found their spots in B16 and B17 and got in line. Once onboard, they found an empty row, and Jules took the window. She always loved being in the window seat. Rick took the aisle and figured they'd get the entire row to themselves. He was right, and not long after they sat down, the flight attendant closed the door and announced that boarding was complete.

Rick used some of his miles to get online, opened his MacBook, and reserved a rental car from Hertz. He was a Hertz Gold member, which meant that when they landed, they could go directly to the car and pick one without standing in line. They drove straight to the courthouse and found a parking spot. After completing the paperwork, they were handed their marriage license. Rick texted the woman he had found online to officiate their wedding and told her they were in town and could meet her around 5:00 p.m. in the hotel lobby. Everything was going as planned.

They couldn't check in at the hotel until after 3:00 p.m., so they headed to downtown Nashville. Rick found a parking spot on 3rd Avenue, and they walked up the street to Broadway. Even though it wasn't quite noon yet, Broadway was hopping. Every single bar had a live band performing. The energy in Nashville was like no other place on the planet. Some of the world's best musicians performed in those little downtown honky-tonks just for tips. Half of them were studio musicians.

"Look, Rick, Boot Barn!" exclaimed Jules like a little kid.

"I see it. Let's go check it out."

Jules already knew what boots she wanted. She had seen them online and was pulling Rick as she skipped toward the store. She took off like a rocket toward the women's boot section once he let her hand go. As Rick walked along the rows of boots, he spotted the cowboy hats. He noticed a really nice Justin star hat, found his size, and tried it on. It was perfect. He kept it on as he looked for the pair of alligator boots he had seen on Jules' phone. After finding the section with his size, he looked up and down the shelves and finally spotted them.

Square-toed boots had become popular. Rick wasn't sure what to think of them. He had grown up wearing Justin

Ropers, but they seemed to be scarce these days. After he tried on the gator boots and looked in the mirror, he was sold.

Jules came bouncing down the aisle in her blue tasseled boots. She looked like an angel.

"I love that hat, Rick. That's a winner."

"I see you found your boots. Let's get you a hat to go with those," said Rick.

He looked at all the hats and knew she'd look good in any hat on the wall. He handed her a nice straw Ariat hat, and it fit her perfectly.

"I love it," said Jules.

They went to the counter, paid for the hats and boots, and placed their shoes in bags. Since they were still near their rental car, Rick walked around the corner and put the shoes back inside the car while Jules stood in front of the window of the Whiskey Bent salon, watching a band play country songs. Rick returned shortly, and they walked down Broadway toward Tootsies. Rick had spent a lot of time in Nashville and was familiar with some of the folklore. They stopped at each bar and listened to each band for a few minutes. Once they reached Tootsies and walked in, Rick shared a bit of the history of Tootsies with Jules.

"Many years ago, the Ryman Auditorium, which sits directly behind Tootsies, was the original Grand Ole Opry. The back door of Tootsies is adjacent to the side door of the Opry stage, and back in the day, when a country star would finish playing a few songs at the Opry, they would exit that side door, step into Tootsies, and sit in with the house band," said Rick.

"Wow, that's cool. Is that what all these photos on the wall are for?" asked Jules.

"Yep. Look, there's George Jones' photo."

Jules took out her iPhone and snapped a picture of *The Possum* for Possum. After listening to a few songs by the band, Rick tipped them, and they crossed the street, walking the other way down Broadway. They stopped at Jason Aldean's bar and got a couple of Heineken 0.0's. The bar was lively, and Jules asked Rick to take her picture several times, as well as asking some strangers to take a picture of her and Rick. She was having the time of her life.

The next stop was Garth Brooks' new place. Jules had seen a documentary on Netflix about it. The bar seemed to have a bit of an identity crisis. Garth was supposed to be country, but the vibe with the palm trees felt more like Jimmy Buffett. Rick liked some of Garth's music but didn't care for the man himself. To Rick, Garth seemed disingenuous. After reading an article where George Strait said Garth wasn't one of them, it sealed the deal for Rick. There was speculation that Strait never said that, and according to Snopes, it wasn't true, but Rick didn't much believe fact-checkers anymore. If George never said a bad word about anyone, Rick thought, even if it wasn't true, he tried to watch a couple of episodes of that documentary, but every other scene had Garth crying, and it was too much for Rick to handle; he never watched another.

"Let's get out of here," said Rick.

They walked down the street, and Jules spotted a bar called Chiefs across from them, just past 3rd Avenue where they had parked.

"Look, Chief's. Aw, I miss Chief," she said.

"Me too, Jules. Let's go to the roof. That's where Morgan Wallen had infamously thrown a chair off the roof and almost hit a cop and got arrested."

Rick loved Morgan's music and felt like he was the real deal. His new favorite country artist was Zach Top, though, and when they walked through the door of Chiefs, his song *I Never Lie* was playing on the speakers as a new band was setting up.

They hung out and listened to the band play a few songs.

"Wanna go find a skirt?" asked Rick.

"Yeah, let's do it."

They walked back to the rental car and headed to Opry Mills, a massive shopping mall next to the hotel where they were getting married. They looked around but couldn't find the right skirt Jules wanted, and someone suggested they try The Mall at Green Hills, so they drove over. After browsing a couple of stores, Jules found the perfect skirt, and Rick also found a black shirt to wear for the ceremony. They had no time to arrange for a photographer, so Rick figured he could take several selfies and ask a stranger to take photos as well. Jules wanted to get her makeup done professionally, so she stepped into MAC while Rick settled himself at a coffee shop to wait. After about forty-five minutes, Jules texted Rick that she was almost done. He strolled over and was blown away by how beautiful she looked.

"I have a surprise for you," said Jules.

"Really? What is it?" asked Rick.

"When I was getting my makeup done one of the girls who works there overheard me telling the woman doing my makeup that we were getting married and didn't have a photographer. She said she was getting off work at 4:00 p.m. and could do it. Besides working at MAC, she's a part-time professional photographer. She said she'd do it for a hundred bucks. She just wanted to help."

"That's awesome Jules!"

"Yeah, I told her we were meeting the officiant at 4:00 p.m. and she said she'd be there too."

"Wow, that is great news. It's all coming together. Let's go check in at the hotel."

Rick dropped off Jules at the lobby and parked the car. By the time he walked back, she had checked in and secured a free upgrade. She was good at those things. Rick kept a running list of all the upgrades she had gotten over the years, it was up to one hundred thirty-five. By the time they got to their room and changed clothes, it was time to meet the officiant and the photographer.

"Nice to meet y'all. I'm Rick, and this is Jules. We're getting married on the Delta Riverboat. I hope y'all don't mind going on a boat ride."

"That's cool," said the photographer as the officiant nodded in agreement.

They all walked down to the ticket booth for the boats.

"Four tickets please. We're getting married on the boat."

The woman selling tickets was shocked. She told them that no one had ever gotten married on the little boat and that she'd need to contact the main office to get permission. She stepped away and came back a few minutes later.

"I'm sorry but corporate says you have to pre-arrange ahead of time to rent the entire boat."

Jules looked devastated. The captain overheard what the ticket saleslady said and walked up.

"If y'all don't mind other people being on the boat, I have no problem with it."

"Thank you so much!" said Rick.

Rick, Jules, the photographer, and the officiant sat in the front half of the boat with Rick and Jules on the bow. Five other people sat in the rear half where the captain was. At first, no one knew what was happening as the captain gave his spiel. At the end of his announcement, he said,

"Ladies and gentlemen, we've never done this before, but we are going to pause the trip for a couple of minutes under our famous Ficus tree, and those two on the bow are getting married. Is everyone okay with that?"

Everyone's eyes lit up, and they all wore huge smiles. Rick and Jules held hands while the photographer snapped away. When they reached the Ficus tree, Rick and Jules pulled out their phones. Rick read the vows he had written on the plane, then Jules did the same.

The officiant did her thing and at the end, she said, "By the power vested in me by the state of Tennessee, I now pronounce you husband and wife. You can kiss the bride."

Rick and Jules kissed each other and hugged tightly, while everyone on the boat applauded, including the captain. They continued down the river, and Jules couldn't stop smiling. When they stepped off the boat, everyone congratulated them. Rick thanked the captain for being so accommodating. They headed up to the room and stepped out on the balcony. The view was breathtaking. Rick made dinner reservations at the Old Hickory Steakhouse.

"Now what, Mr. Waters?" asked Jules

"You know what, Mrs. Waters? You can leave your boots on," said Rick.

They made love and held each other tighter than ever before. They were both completely and utterly in love.

CHAPTER

FOUR

P ossum sat down at the AVID editing desk in the trailer on the set. He had edited before with Final Cut Pro and knew there would be a learning curve for the new software. He had just gotten started when he heard a knock on the door.

"Come in."

"Hey Possum," said Johnie.

"You made it! How was the drive? Is Clay here?"

"The drive was great. That Entegra Aspire Rick bought floats down the highway. Clay was a few miles behind me in Gary's Prevost. He should be here soon. Richard showed me where to park and plug in. He got some fifty-amp adapters for the huge generators. Whatcha doing?" asked Johnie.

"I'm trying to learn this AVID editing software to edit the movie we shot in Egypt."

"Wow, that's awesome. Where's Rick?"

"He and Jules flew to Nashville for a quick getaway

before we start filming here. The production crew won't be here for a few days."

"Typical Rick," said Johnie.

"Oh, by the way, Gary reserved you and Clay a room at the Windsor Court in New Orleans. I can give you a ride after I'm done here. I'm sure you could use a few days out of the RV."

"I have my Bronco behind the motorhome."

"Oh, that's right. I forgot. Okay, you can head over there whenever you want to."

"Alright, I'll chill out until Clay gets here, and then I'll drive us both over there."

"Okay, Johnie. Good to see you."

"You too, Possum."

Possum spun his chair around and dove back into the video lessons for the AVID software. Clay arrived thirty minutes later and stopped in to say hi to Possum, then he and Johnie headed into New Orleans. After they checked in, Johnie texted Rick.

Rick, we made it to New Orleans. I have Chief at the hotel in his travel cage.

Thanks, Johnie. We'll be back the day after tomorrow. Thanks for taking care of the Chief.

My pleasure.

Rick and Jules sat at a table the manager set up for them near the edge of the balcony at the Old Hickory Steakhouse. From that table, they could see the entire grounds of the atrium. Before their meals arrived, a beautiful LED light show was displayed over the dancing fountains. Jules took a video with her phone.

Rick ordered a sixteen-ounce aged ribeye with a baked potato and crispy Brussels sprouts. Jules went for the eight-ounce Wagyu filet with creamed spinach and mashed potatoes. They shared the sides and loved every single bite. They promised the waiter they'd visit again every time they were in Nashville and ask for his section. After dinner, they took a stroll around the atrium. It was amazing to be inside, yet it felt like they were outside. The flowers and plants were astonishing. When they arrived at the room, they sat on the balcony, taking in the view and chatting. It was a perfect ending to a perfect day.

Rick awoke to the sound of someone talking in the hallway. He got up, let Jules sleep in, and walked down to the Starbucks in the center of the atrium. He got both himself and Jules some tall coffees and returned. Jules was in the shower when he arrived. Rick took the coffees out to the balcony and waited for Jules to finish her shower.

"Good morning, wifey," said Rick.

Jules smiled and took her coffee.

"Good morning, hubby. What's on the agenda today?"

"We need to take our signed wedding license down to the courthouse and make it official. After that, we can do whatever you'd like."

Jules put her hand to her heart and smiled. She looked down at her ring and was so happy. She was married to Rick and felt a sense of contentment and peace.

"Can we go to the Grand Ole Opry tonight?" asked Jules.

"Sure, let me see who's playing."

Rick looked at his iPhone, then nearly jumped out of his skin, startling Jules "Holy shit! Zach Top is playing tonight. I'm booking tickets now!"

Rick booked seats up front and center. He was thrilled. They had already seen Zach once at the Houston Livestock and Rodeo, but this time they would be much closer. Rick felt like Zach was the heir apparent to George Strait.

"After we drop off the wedding license, why don't we drive around down by Music Row and do some sightseeing?" asked Rick.

"That would be awesome," replied Jules.

They ended up getting the same parking spot at the courthouse, and there was no one in line when they got to the window. Rick handed the woman their signed paperwork. She congratulated them, and they left.

"No turning back now, Jules."

"I wouldn't change a thing!"

Rick drove back toward downtown and pointed out a few sights on Music Row. "Siri, play 'Good Beer and Country Music' by Zach Top," said Rick.

"Good Beer and Country Music by Zach Top now playing on Apple Music," replied Siri.

Rick and Jules drove all around Nashville and listened to Zach's debut album three times.

"Damn, that boy's good," said Rick.

"I know. He has that '90s sound down pat."

Rick turned onto Demonbreun Street and then down Music Square West.

"Look, Jules, there's RCA Studio B. Roy Orbison and Elvis recorded there."

"Wow, that's cool. There's so much history down here," said Jules.

After they saw most of the cool sights, they headed back to the Opryland Hotel. Rick played the Zach Top album again in the room. He changed into his jeans and boots, and so did Jules.

"Wanna get a little bite to eat, then head over to the Opry, Jules?"

"Sure. How about that Jack Daniels place? They have comfort food."

Rick opened his phone and looked at the menu.

"Oh, hell yeah! I'm getting BBQ Mac and Cheese. They also have Shrimp and Grits."

"Sold!" exclaimed Jules.

They walked through the hotel's maze, got lost twice, and eventually found the Jack Daniels restaurant. The food lived up to the hype and they were glad to be walking to the Grand Ole Opry to work off their meals. When they arrived at the Opry, they made their way to the front, and when they reached their seats, Jules was blown away by how close they were. She could read the brand name of the microphone at the center of the stage. Several acts performed, and they were all spot on. The sound in the Grand Ole Opry was spectacular. Rick had a permanent smile on his face.

"Ladies and gentlemen, please welcome to the stage, Zach Top," said the M.C."

Rick stood up and applauded vigorously. Zack stepped forward, wearing Wranglers and a white, blue, and green striped Mo Betta western shirt. The band immediately kicked off with Zack's hit, *"I Never Lie."* Rick let out a loud holler. He was also impressed by how good a guitar player Zack was, as he played most of the solos in his songs. Zack came back for one more song and closed out the show with *Sounds Like The Radio.* Rick zoomed in with his iPhone camera on the headstock of Zack's acoustic guitar and took a photo of it. When he looked at it, he saw it was a Thompson. After googling it, he found out it was a Preston Thompson acoustic, made in Sisters, Oregon, which made sense because Zack grew up not too far from there in Sunnyside, Washington.

After the show, Rick and Jules strolled back to the Opryland Hotel. Rick couldn't stop singing the songs Zach performed, which made Jules laugh. As they strolled back, Rick's phone vibrated. It was a text from Possum.

Hey, Rick, the production company arrived from Germany this afternoon. No hurry back; we're shooting a night scene, mostly with extras.

We're headed back in the morning. See ya midday.

"Who was that? asked Jules.

"Possum. He said the crew has arrived, and they will be shooting some B-roll night shots tomorrow. Are you ready to be transformed into a Voodoo Queen?"

"I can't wait!"

"I'm not tired; you wanna go hear some music downtown?"

"That would be great," said Jules.

They walked to the parking lot instead of the room and drove down to 2nd Avenue. It was incredibly busy downtown, so Rick parked in the garage on 5th Avenue. They walked up 5th to Broadway and turned right, then saw a line of people entering a place on 4th Avenue. Curiosity got the best of them, so they approached. The people were in line to get into Morgan Wallen's new place. Rick looked at Jules, and she shrugged as if to say, "*Why not?*" They moved rather fast, and it only took them ten minutes to get inside.

"I wonder why there is a line tonight?" Rick asked aloud.

The guy in front of him overheard Rick, turned around, and said,

"The rumor is that Morgan is gonna sit in with the house band tonight."

"Wow, cool, thanks for the tip," said Rick.

When they stepped inside, the house band was already on stage playing classic country. Rick and Jules squeezed into a spot at the bar adjacent to the stage. The venue was well-designed, featuring a huge stage along one wall, with massive line array speakers suspended from the ceiling and subwoofers positioned on the floor. The sound was superb. The bartender leaned closer to them to talk over the volume of the band.

"What can I getcha?"

"Two Heineken 0.0's," said Rick.

The bartender opened the two bottles and poured them two glasses of ice water. Rick paid cash instead of starting a tab. After about seven songs, the band took a break, and the house music came on. About fifteen minutes later, all the lights went down, and it was almost pitch black. Rick could see some movement on stage, but it was too dark to see what was happening. The lights were still down, and the sound of a lap steel guitar started playing the intro to *"Up Down."* The crowd erupted. When the chorus kicked off, the house lights blazed a super-bright white, illuminating the crowd as Morgan jumped up and down, singing. The place was on fire.

Morgan thanked everyone for coming to his new venue and then kicked off *"Whiskey Glasses."* He was right on the money with the vocals, and the band was tight. He played hit after hit and took a break. Rick took the opportunity to hit the bathroom while Jules held their spot at the bar.

A few minutes after Rick walked away, a belligerent, drunk guy pushed himself up to the bar beside Jules.

"Damn girl, you're hot. Let me buy you a drink."

"I'm with someone and I don't drink," replied Jules, trying to ignore him.

"I don't see anyone," he said as he tried to put his arm around her.

She pushed his arm away.

"I told you I'm with someone. Now fuck off!"

Rick was walking up and saw something going on. As he got close, the guy said, "Fucking spic!" as he pushed Jules in the forehead with his pointer finger.

Without even thinking, Rick closed his fist and hit him square in the face, knocking him to the ground. Two of his buddies jumped in and grabbed Rick by the shoulder, spinning him around. One swung at him, and he ducked; then Rick head-butted him. The other one reached for Rick and elbowed him in the throat. An off-duty cop who was working as a bouncer stepped in and grabbed Rick by the collar, pulling him toward the entrance. Rick tried to explain as all three guys were either bleeding or on the floor. The cop threw Rick in the back of his squad car before he could explain that it was self-defense. He called for backup, and a second cop came, moving Rick to it. Jules ran outside trying to explain. The cops weren't listening. Luckily, Rick had given Jules the keys because his Wranglers were too tight. Rick was gone and out of sight within minutes.

"Where are you taking him?" asked Jules.

"Jail, duh!" said the smartass cop.

"What jail?"

"Nashville Detention Center on James Robertson. He will be booked there. He'll have his first appearance in the morning."

"What does that mean?" asked Jules.

"It means he'll see the judge in the morning."

"What about those other three guys? One was harassing me," said Jules.

"Ma'am, all I know is I saw your boyfriend hitting those guys. He can tell it to the judge," said the cop.

Jules ran back into the bar. The three guys had moved to the rear of the bar. The bartender got her attention.

"Miss, miss. I saw everything. If you need me to testify on behalf of your boyfriend, I will. Those guys deserved everything they got. Follow me," he said as he pointed to the camera directly behind him, facing Jules.

Jules walked with him to a back room, where he asked the security guard to email her a copy of the footage after instructing him to rewind it to the perfect moment. They all watched the screen. There was no sound, but it was clearly visible that the guy was pushing his finger against Jules' forehead. That was assault. The bartender wrote his cell number on a piece of a Post-it note.

"If you need a bail bondsman, try Tennessee Bonding Company on 3rd Avenue. He'll probably only get a thousand-dollar cash bail in the morning anyway," said the bartender.

"He has to spend the night in jail?" asked Jules as her eyes welled up.

"I'm afraid so, ma'am. The judge will see him in the morning and set bail. I'm having those guys thrown out. My guess is that they won't even press charges. If they do, I got your back. As a matter of fact, I'm gonna go tell the one that was harassing you that I have them on camera. I can almost guarantee they won't show up to press charges. The case will get dismissed. I'm sorry y'all had to go through this tonight. Please don't hold it against Morgan's venue. Sometimes dickheads like to start trouble and that can happen anywhere."

"I know. We had a great time until that happened. Thanks for your help," said Jules.

She left and walked to the rental car, then headed to the detention center. The lady behind the desk told her there was nothing she could do and that 'first appearance' was at 8:00 a.m., and she could come back then to sit in the waiting room. Jules was sniffling, trying not to cry, and could do nothing but return to the hotel. She was so upset that she wanted to call Possum, but it was after 1:00 a.m. by the time she got back to her room. Unable to sleep, she Googled lawyers in the Nashville area and set her alarm for 7:00 a.m. She undressed, lay down on the bed, and worried about Rick. She knew he was a tough guy, though, and could handle himself. It wasn't the first time he'd been in jail. Hell, he'd been in a Mexican prison once. Eventually, she fell asleep after tossing and turning for what felt like forever. She woke up when her phone started ringing. She looked at her phone and saw it was 8:45 a.m. Her alarm hadn't gone off, and she had overslept. It was Rick calling.

"Hey, baby, I'm out. The judge set my bond at a thousand dollars. I just used my debit card."

"Are you okay, Rick? I'm so sorry. I overslept. My damn alarm didn't go off."

"No problem, Jules. I'm gonna walk across the street. There's a food truck there. I'm gonna grab some coffee. You can pick me up there and we can go to breakfast."

"I have a lot to tell you. I'm leaving now."

"Okay, baby. Drive safe."

Jules didn't take Rick's advice and drove like she was in NASCAR race. She felt guilty for oversleeping. She had accidentally set her alarm for p.m. instead of a.m. When she arrived, Rick was sitting on a curb, sipping coffee. She put on a brave face as she pulled up and rolled down the window.

"Need a ride, Jailbird?"

"Sure, stranger," replied Rick.

Jules slid over and let Rick drive. Her hands were still shaking and Rick noticed.

"Honey, it was fine. I slept pretty well. I never even went to general population because I got in so late. I was in the holding cell area until I saw the judge. Only two other people came in last night. I'm starving. Our flight isn't until 11:40 a.m. and there is a great restaurant over by Vanderbilt on Hillsboro."

Rick parked on the street, and they walked over to the Pancake Pantry. It had been a Nashville tradition for as long as Rick could remember. Since they were so early and it was a weekday, it didn't take long to get a table. They sat at a two-top by the window, and Rick didn't even open the menu. He knew what he wanted. Jules decided to get the Chocolate Sin, which was three crepe-style pancakes with chocolate ganache. The waitress walked up to the table.

"Hi, I'm Stephanie, I'll be taking care of you. Coffee?"

They both responded yes in unison.

"I think we are ready to order, too," said Rick.

"Okay, go right ahead," said the waitress as she took out her notepad.

"I'll have the Smoky Mountain Buckwheat Pancakes with a side of scrambled eggs with cheddar and she'll take the Chocolate Sin Pancakes."

"Sounds good," she said as she poured their coffee.

"I can't believe how relaxed you are, Rick."

"Ain't no biggie."

"Oh, I wanna show you something," said Jules as she opened her email and showed Rick the video the security guard had sent her from Morgan Wallen's bar.

Rick watched it and just shook his head. "He's lucky all I did was break his nose. Fucking punk."

They finished their breakfast and headed to the hotel to get ready for the flight. They arrived early and checked in. Once in their seats, Jules squeezed Rick's arm.

"Thank you for protecting me."

"Thank you for marrying me," said Rick as he winked at her.

CHAPTER
FIVE

Rick and Jules went straight from the New Orleans airport to the set at the Bayou Sauvage National Wildlife Refuge. It wasn't that they were worried about being late for the shoot that day; they probably weren't even needed. They just wanted to see Chief. It had been too long since they had seen him, and Johnie had him on the set in his travel cage in Rick's motorhome. Rick pulled up next to the motorhome, and Johnie opened the door and stepped out.

"How was Nashville?"

"An adventure, that's for sure. I'll tell all y'all over dinner. Where's Chief?"

"Inside," replied Johnie.

Rick and Jules rushed inside, and when Chief spotted them, he flew off his PVC perch into Rick's chest.

"Hey buddy, we missed you," said Rick.

Jules kissed his beak as he bounced up and down, raising

his crest and cooing. Rick stroked his back for a while before passing him to Jules, where he snuggled under her chin. They spent the next thirty minutes playing with Chief. It was a wonderful, loving reunion. Rick wanted to talk to Possum, so he stepped over to the editing trailer and knocked.

"Come on in," yelled Possum.

"Hey, Amigo, how's it going?"

"Good. I'm getting the hang of this editing software. How was Nashville?"

"Well, I can't say uneventful. I spent last night in jail."

"What?!"

"Yeah, some punk was harassing Jules at the new Morgan Wallen bar, and I kicked his ass. A cop who was moonlighting there as a bouncer took me as the aggressor. It's no biggie; it'll all turn out okay. Jules got a video of the guy poking her in the head with his finger. He called her a spic. Big mistake."

"Fucking scumbag," replied Possum.

"I hear y'all are gonna be shooting some B-roll tonight with a bunch of zombie extras."

"Yeah, y'all don't have to be here unless you wanna watch. I'm sure you're tired from being in jail."

"I slept pretty good, surprisingly."

"That's good. I'm glad y'all are back. Gary's over in his Prevost if you wanna talk to him."

Hey, can we all go to dinner tonight in town? I wanna tell you all something and don't wanna have to say it five times," said Rick.

"Sure, talk to Gary, and I'll be there, whatever y'all

decide. We should be wrapped for the day by 6:30 p.m. or so."

"Sounds good. Happy editing."

Rick walked over to Gary's Prevost bus and knocked on the door. He opened it and peeked his head out.

"Hey, you're back."

"Yep. Listen, I have something cool to share with y'all. Can we all get together at some restaurant where we can have a private room after the shoot tonight?" asked Rick.

"Sure, what ya thinking? Cajun? Steak?"

"Don't matter. Actually, we had steaks two nights ago. Let's go with Cajun."

"Let me think," said Gary as he pulled out his iPhone. "How about Cochon's?"

"Yeah, that'll work. They offer private dining, and their famous five-course *Feed Me* menu. Great thinking," said Rick.

"Who should I invite?"

"Just us, no one from the crew. So, me, you, Jules, Possum, Jonnie, and Clay."

"What about Chief?"

"Ha-ha, I wish! Wouldn't he like that?!"

"Okay, I'll call and make the reservation."

"Thanks Gary."

Rick returned to the motorhome and Jules was sitting on the couch playing with Chief.

"Hey Jules, we're going to dinner tonight at this great restaurant called Cochon's. I wanna tell everyone that we got married. Well, let's show them. I'll say something and give you the cue, hold up your left hand, and show off your rings."

"Great idea, Rick. I'll put the wedding band away for now. They've all seen my engagement ring already."

The extras began to arrive, and Richard had set up a team of makeup artists to transform them into frightening-looking zombies. They were all instructed to wear dirty, ripped street clothes. Five makeup artists were working with all the extras. Rick watched as they were transformed. It was incredibly fascinating. Some were just bloody, and some had exposed bones and broken ribs showing. It was magic what the make up artists did.

The cameraman, grips, and the rest of the crew set up lights, cables, and everything they needed for the scene. Possum came out and spoke to Paul, the assistant director, about the shot. He was waiting for the golden hour, when the sun is just above the horizon and casts shadows on the faces. When he felt it was perfect he called the extras to get into position.

"When I call action, I want you to walk toward the camera as if you see a freshly made butter biscuit and you haven't eaten for a couple of days. I need you to bite into the air over and over, as if you were eating something. The rest of you hang back until I wave toward you, then walk forward with a limping motion and flail your arms occasionally. I eventually want all of you to pass the camera and exit the shot. Does everyone understand?" asked Possum. They all nodded and murmured yes.

The AD called for quiet on the set.

"We have sound. Rolling now," said the cameraman.

"And action!" said Possum.

The zombies did what Possum requested perfectly.

"Cut! Let's go again. Back to one," said Possum.

They shot the same scene four more times, and Possum was satisfied.

"Okay let's move to the travel trailer scene," said Possum.

In this scene, zombies try to break into an old travel trailer parked at the refuge. It is a retro-looking RV that the set designer found at a used RV sales center in Slidell. The paint is faded, and there is considerable rust on the frame and hitch. He purchased it for five hundred dollars. A family of three is inside, and the father has a shotgun. They have rigged squibs in the chest and head of some zombies, and when they ripped the door open, the father blasted the first zombie, and the squib exploded, sending him to the ground. Then he shot the second one in the head, and the squib sprayed blood all over the side of the trailer. That zombie wobbled a little before falling to his knees, then forward to the ground.

"Cut!"

It was a perfect scene. The crew cleaned the blood off the side of the trailer, and everyone went back to one. This time, they put a green hood over the zombie that was shot in the head and hung a green screen over the trailer. They reshot the same scene from a different angle. In post-production, with the right cuts, it would appear that the zombie's head was blown off. This film had a much bigger budget and effects team than the first movie Possum had directed. He planned to have fun with it, and since it was a horror/thriller, he always had the styles of Quentin Tarantino and Robert Rodriguez in the back of his mind. After two retakes, Possum was pleased with the shots and called the day's shooting over. He went to his trailer with Paul, and they watched the dailies. The cameras they were using were so much better than the ones they had used in Egypt. It looked rich.

Rick and Jules took Chief with his travel cage back to the hotel to relax for a while before dinner. When Rick arrived, they had to pay a hundred and fifty-dollar refundable pet deposit. He didn't mind. Once they got to the room, Rick put together the portable PVC perch he had built. He placed it by the huge window, and Chief seemed content enjoying looking at the city below through the window.

Rick received a text from Gary stating that he and Possum were heading to the restaurant a little early to ensure the private dining room was ready. Rick let him know they'd be there by 7:00 p.m. Rick walked down to the lobby and asked the lady working at the front desk if there was a grocery store nearby. She told him Rouses Market was about a fifteen-minute walk over on Poydras Street. Rick decided to walk instead of taking the Jeep since it was a nice night out and he loved the city so much.

As he walked toward the market, he was approached by several beggars and homeless individuals. He never knew if someone begging truly needed money for food or was just trying to score cash for drugs. This saddened him. Rick was always generous about helping others, but when he saw young, able-bodied men begging for money instead of work-ing, he would ignore them. Once he reached the grocery store, he found the produce section and bought some red grapes for Chief. They were his favorite, and Rick loved to pamper him. He also brought home some unsalted peanuts in the shell and a box of wooden tongue depressors. Those would keep him busy while they had dinner. Chief could spend hours destroying tongue depressors. He never grew bored with them.

When he returned to the hotel, Jules had already showered and had bathed Chief as well. He needed one badly. To Rick, Chief always looked like a drowned rat when he was soaking wet.

"Hey, boy, I have something for you," said Rick, passing Chief a red grape.

He held it with his little foot and peeled the skin off it. He always ate them the same way. He would peel the outer skin, then eat the grape from the inside out. When it was time to head to the restaurant, Rick put a half dozen tongue depressors in the empty food bowl of Chief's travel cage. He immediately went to town, ripping it apart and throwing the small shards of wood everywhere. It would make a mess, but it also kept him quiet.

When they arrived at the restaurant, the hostess showed them to the private dining room, where the rest of the gang was already sitting. Rick and Jules took their seats at the large round table. Gary let the waiter know that everyone had arrived and that he could begin the first course. Rick ordered a Guinness 0 and Jules got an Athletic Wave. Rick poured his Guinness into a tall, cold mug that the waiter gave him and used his butter knife to clink on the side of the glass to get everyone's attention. That was Jules' cue to put on her wedding band, so she pulled it out of her purse, put her hand under the table, and slid it on her finger.

"As you know, I brought you all here to tell you something. You also know that Jules and I just returned from

Nashville. We stayed at the Opryland Hotel. We even saw Zach Top at the Grand Ole Opry one night and Morgan Wallen at his new bar. You also know that I got arrested for fighting. No biggie. But what you don't know. Well, instead of telling you, Jules, show them," said Rick.

Jules pulled her left hand from under the table, held it up and started waving it. Possum's jaw hit the floor and everyone's eyes got wide.

"Y'all got married?!" asked Gary.

"Congratulations," said Possum, followed by everyone else.

Gary stood up and said,

"Now this is a party! Waiter!" he exclaimed.

The waiter came over, and Gary told him what had just transpired. The waiter returned with several bottles of Crystal Champagne and a bottle of Prima Pavé Grand Cuvée non-alcoholic Champagne for Rick and Jules. Soon after, they all toasted to Rick and Jules' union, and the first course arrived. They ate, drank, and celebrated for several hours. The waiter delivered a special dessert for the newlyweds, and it was the end to a perfect night.

Rick awoke to a text from Possum.

Have you spoken to Paul? He's not answering his texts. I'm at the set and he's supposed to be here. We are supposed to film some gross close-up scenes of zombies eating people's guts.

No, I just woke up, actually. I'll knock on his door. Hang on.

Rick knocked on Paul's door, then stuck his ear to the door to see if he could hear anything. He tipped the housekeeper ten bucks to open his door. It was empty, and it looked like he hadn't made his bed. Rick returned to his room and texted Possum back.

He's not in there. Maybe he got hammered last night. He's probably sleeping it off. I know he and his boyfriend have been together for a little over three years. Do you have his number?

No, but he's staying at the same hotel as the crew. I'll call the front desk.

Good idea. Jules and I will head your way soon. Peace.

Rick brewed a pot of coffee and hopped into the shower. Jules sneaked in behind him and washed his back. One scrub led to another, and soon they were in bed making love. Afterward, they lay in the glow of love. Rick ordered some croissants from room service, and they got dressed while they waited. Chief nibbled on a tiny piece of Jules' croissant before they left for the refuge.

"You be a good boy," said Rick as he filled up his food bowl with pellets and freshened his water.

For a cockatoo, Chief was remarkably quiet compared to most. Rick always left the TV or radio on to keep him company. However, as long as he had plenty of things to play with, he nearly never made a peep. Rick pulled the Jeep around, and Jules climbed inside. It was an overcast day, and Rick knew it would be a good day for Possum to film the close-ups of the gut-eating scenes as there would be no shadows from the sun. Only a few of the extras agreed to shoot those scenes and received extra compensation because Possum used animal entrails for realism. It was kinda nasty. They mostly came from cows and pigs. Possum learned of the practice from Richard, who had been on the set before the SAG crew went on strike. The new crew just picked up where they left off. On the set were two large box freezers, where the guts were stored. They didn't want anyone getting sick. The entrails came from a local butcher who had a spotless record of cleanliness. Possum had learned that before he took over from the last crew as director, some animal rights activists had stormed onto the set to protest, and it had gotten a little violent. So, now it was a closed set, and everyone who worked on the film, including extras, needed ID. No visitors were allowed on the set and the producer hired security. When Rick turned the corner down to the set, he could see an ambulance and several police vehicles. The entire set entrance was taped off with crime scene tape.

"Oh fuck. Something bad has happened. I hope no one got hurt with one of those damn blood squibs," said Rick.

They both stepped out of the Jeep and Possum told the cop to let them inside the taped area. That's when Rick saw the coroner's van over by the staging area.

"Oh no," he murmured.

Possum walked up and had a horrible look on his face.

"What happened?" asked Rick.

"It's Paul. He's dead."

"What?! How? What happened?" asked Rick.

"As I told you, he never showed up to the set today and wasn't responding to any texts. I had to start filming without him. I asked one of the PAs to pull some animal entrails out of the freezer to thaw out, and when he opened the freezer, he found Paul's body. Rick, someone gutted him and. a huge bite was taken out of his face."

"Oh my God. What the fuck? Some psycho turned into an actual zombie?" asked Rick.

"We have no idea yet. The sheriff's department is sending some detectives to ask everyone questions. They'll be here soon," said Possum.

Rick paced back and forth, feeling extremely upset. He had grown to like Paul ever since they had worked together on the movie in Egypt. Paul was a very likable guy, and Rick didn't care that he was gay. His boyfriend Adam was nice too, and Rick got along well with both of them. Rick put his arms around Jules, and they stepped into his motorhome. A murder on the set was the last thing Rick expected to encounter today.

CHAPTER
SIX

Rick knocked on the door of Adam's hotel room. He didn't answer. The last thing Rick wanted to do was be the one to tell him that Paul had been murdered, but he drew the short straw. The police were still at the scene, and CSI and the detectives were continuing to work on the case. Rick was questioned early on and cleared. The entire gang had rock-solid alibis, as the time of death was sometime the night before, while they were all at the restaurant. Rick got the manager to open the door. Stepping inside, he noticed the bathroom light was on. When he glanced in, he saw blood in the sink.

"Call 911," Rick said to the manager.

Rick looked around the room, ensuring he didn't touch anything. The bed was a mess, and he didn't notice any luggage. He suspected a mix of Paul and Adam's DNA since Paul had been in his room. The blood in the sink might be from shaving, so he didn't want to jump to conclusions, although it appeared more like someone had been cleaning up blood from their hands rather than a simple shaving cut.

Rick and Jules waited in the lobby for the police to arrive. When they did, he explained to them what he had discovered upon entering the room. They immediately called CSI, who arrived about thirty minutes later. Rick stood in the hallway in case they had any questions for him.

The elevator chimed and Adam stepped off.

"What's going on?" asked Adam.

"Where have you been?" asked Rick.

"I went to the gym last night and then to the pool. I fell asleep on a lounge chair. My head is pounding. I don't even remember lying down at the pool. I don't remember anything after the gym. Why are cops in my room?"

"You don't know?" asked Rick.

"Know what?"

"Aw, Adam. I'm sorry to tell you, but Paul was murdered last night."

Adam's mouth dropped open and tears filled his eyes.

"Murdered? How? By who?"

"I can't tell you anything right now. I'm sure the police will want to talk to you. Hang on."

Rick caught the attention of the lead investigator and informed him that Paul had arrived. He whispered to the cop to do a check on Adam's blood for drugs.

"His memory is vague. I think he got roofied last night."

"Thanks for the tip," said the detective.

The detective stepped out and spoke to Adam for a while. Together, they headed to the elevator and went down to the lobby to be interrogated at the station. The CSI team taped off the room, so Rick and Jules left. There was no need to be there.

"That was weird," said Jules.

"I know. He said he woke up in a lounge chair and doesn't know how he got there. Damn, I wonder if he needs a lawyer. I forgot to tell him to ask for one. His alibi will be weak, and because he was Paul's boyfriend, the cops are going to key him. If he ain't involved, he's gonna need representation. Let's got to the station. Can you look online and see what defense attorneys have good reviews?"

Jules opened her phone and found a highly rated lawyer, called him and got him up to speed. She turned off the phone and nodded at Rick.

"He said he'll head down to the station. He needs a twenty-thousand-dollar retainer. Should we do that for him? It's a lot of money," said Jules.

"It is, but I have a gut feeling he's not involved. If he is, I'll back off. Plus, if Adam agrees and I pay for the attorney, we can stay in the loop and find out stuff we may not have prior knowledge of ordinarily. I know we don't know Adam that well, but he seems like a good guy."

"Whatever you think, hubby," said Jules with a grin.

Rick smiled. He liked hearing that. When they arrived at the station, Adam was in the interrogation room with two detectives. The lawyer hadn't arrived yet, and Rick couldn't get to Adam to warn him to stay quiet. He was from Germany and most likely unfamiliar with the U.S. laws and tactics detectives could use in the interrogation room. Rick was wringing his hands when the lawyer finally arrived. Rick introduced himself and told the lawyer that he would be paying the retainer. The chubby southern lawyer had a huge mustache and reminded Rick of a middle-aged Wilford Brimley. He could've been his doppelgänger.

"Get in there. He has no idea that they will try to pin this on him."

The lawyer hustled in and got into the interrogation room.

"That'll be all for now. My client has nothing else to say." Adam was confused.

"Please turn off the camera. I need to speak to my client."

The detectives turned off the camera and reluctantly left the room.

"Adam, my name is Todd Thomas. I'll be defending you."

"Are you a public defender?"

"Hell no. Rick Waters hired me, his wife got me up to speed so far."

"Rick hired you? I barely know him. He is one of the actors or something in the film my boyfriend, Paul, was working on. He was the assistant director. I met Rick a few times in Egypt and spoke to him again today."

Adam broke down and started crying after he said that. The reality of Paul being dead hit him hard.

"What did you tell the cops?" asked Todd.

"I told them I went to the gym last night and then woke up at the pool on a lounge chair outside the gym door."

"I'm only gonna ask you this once. Most lawyers don't care but if I'm going to defend someone, I have to know. Did you have anything to do with Paul's death?"

"God no! I loved him. I still love him. Oh my God, I can't believe he's gone. We were planning a road trip after the film wrapped. It's my first time in the U.S., and we wanted to drive out west and he wanted to show me the Grand Canyon and maybe get married in Vegas," said Adam as his voice cracked and tears streamed down his cheeks.

Todd listened to him and believed him.

"I'm gonna ask you some personal questions now. Okay?"

Adam nodded, wiping the tears away.

"Do you do drugs?"

"Not hard drugs. I occasionally smoke pot, but I haven't had any since I left Germany. I have no idea where to get it here, and it was impossible in Egypt. I rarely smoke anyway. I bet the last time I had any was over three months ago."

"Good. Your accent isn't German, is it?"

"No, I'm from Denmark. I met Paul when he was on vacation in Copenhagen. I was his trainer at the resort gym. I've been a personal trainer for many years."

"I see. I noticed you are quite pumped up. Show me your hands."

"The cops took photos of them," said Adam.

"What is that cut on your right palm?"

"I don't remember how I cut it. Maybe when I was working out. I honestly can't remember."

Todd shook his head and grimaced.

"Okay, let's go back to last night. You said you were at the gym then woke up on a lounge chair. Right?"

"Yes."

"Is that normal for you?

"No. I don't even remember stepping out to the pool. I always do the same workout when possible. I work out, and then immediately after my workout, I go into a sauna or slip into my infrared sauna blanket that I travel with. Since the hotel has a wooden heat sauna, I planned to use that after my workout, but I don't remember going there."

"What's the last thing you remember? Think hard."

Adam took a deep breath.

"I was doing the last set of kettlebell windmills, and I felt dehydrated from going too hard. We have been eating all this fried Cajun food since we got here, so I went extra hard."

Adam rubbed his chin and glanced at the ceiling, trying to remember.

"Then I took a large gulp of my recovery drink in my Yeti bottle. That's honestly all I can recall."

"Yeti, you say?"

"Yeah, Paul got it for me for my birthday. He had it engraved for me. It's one of those stainless steel thirty-six-ounce chug cups. I use it all the time."

"Where is it now?"

"That's a good question. I have no idea. Maybe in the gym still?"

"I'll have someone look for it," said Todd.

"Hang on a second. I'm gonna go talk to the detective. Did they read you your Miranda Rights?"

"Yeah. They were pretty intense with me."

"That's what they do. It's a good thing I got here. They want a confession."

"But I didn't do it," said Adam.

"They don't care. If they believe you did it, they will pressure you until you confess. I've seen it more times than you can imagine," said Todd as he stepped out of the room.

Todd found the detectives.

"Is he a suspect or just a person of interest? Do you plan on charging him?"

The black detective, named Jones, looked at his white partner, and they both shrugged.

"Not yet. He is a strong person of interest. We are still waiting for the forensic results to come back. We'll decide then," said Jones.

"Since he's not under arrest, my client will be leaving now," said Todd.

"Tell him not to leave town."

Todd smirked and clicked his tongue.

"Let's go. We're outta here," said Todd as he cracked open the interrogation room.

They walked out into the lobby, where Rick and Jules were still sitting.

"Mr. Waters. I will take the case. Here's my card. Call my secretary, and she can arrange for the wire for the retainer. Adam, you can't return to your hotel. It's a crime scene now. Do you have anywhere you can stay?"

"I don't even have my wallet or luggage. It's all at the hotel," said Adam.

"There was no luggage in the room when I looked inside."

"That's weird. My Under Armor duffle bag was on the luggage rack by the dresser. It has my initials embroidered on it. My portable infrared sauna blanket was sitting on the edge of the bed. Was it still there?" asked Adam.

"The bed was a mess, and the room was empty. Where was your wallet?"

"I always make my bed. I learned that in the military. My wallet was sitting by the phone on the nightstand."

"There was nothing there. You're welcome to join us and stay in Paul's room. The police have cleared it. If you're not comfortable with that, we can get you another room."

"Thank you. I'll stay in Paul's room. Maybe I can still smell him on the pillow," said Adam as he put his head in his hands.

Rick patted him on the back.

"I'm so sorry for your loss. We'll figure this out. I promise."

Adam followed Jules out to the Jeep and proceeded to the hotel. The police had fingerprinted the room and checked it for DNA. They had removed all of Paul's belongings and released the room back to the hotel.

"Get some rest. If you get hungry, order something from room service. Later on, Jules can take you shopping, and you can get some clothes and a new suitcase. If you need anything, here's my cell number, or we're only three doors down in room 1609," said Rick as he handed Adam his business card.

"Why are you being so nice to me, Mr. Waters?" asked Adam.

"Call me Rick. Mr. Waters is my father. I liked Paul and I like you too. It's the least I can do. My gut instinct tells me you had nothing to do with Paul's death. I always trust my gut."

"I didn't. I swear!"

"I believe you, Adam. Get some rest and we'll chat later."

"Thanks, Rick."

Rick and Jules stepped into their room.

"Do you really think he's innocent?" asked Jules.

"I do. I've seen them together. They looked happy. I know you can never know what goes on behind closed doors, but my instinct is telling me he had absolutely nothing to do with it."

"I hope you're right, Rick. Adam is a nice guy. I still can't believe Paul is dead. We just saw him yesterday," said Jules.

"I know. It's a shocker," said Rick as he hugged Jules for a long time.

"I'm gonna call the lawyer's secretary and get the wire info, call Possum and see what's going on at the set."

Rick made his calls and then logged into NEXUS to see if he could find any information on Adam Olsen. After an exhaustive search, he discovered that Adam was clean. He grew up in Denmark and established a reputation as a personal trainer. He moved to Germany three years ago and took some time off from the gym in Frankfurt to go to Egypt and then the US. He had no criminal record whatsoever.

"All we can do now is wait for forensics. Possum said they had to stop filming until the police released the crime scene. He said it's organized chaos down there."

"What should we do?" asked Jules.

"We should go for a bike ride. I need to blow off some steam and get my head on straight," said Rick.

"I like the way you think, Mr. Waters."

"Thank you, Mrs. Waters," replied Rick.

That was the first time Jules thought about being Mrs. Waters. She hadn't decided if she was changing her last name yet. Her last name was Castro, and she liked Waters.

She was just happy that Rick wasn't putting any pressure on her to change her last name. She'd have to give it some thought.

"Jules, there's a great trail down by the Mississippi River called the Crescent Trail. It runs about twenty-four miles. We can take it up to Bywater and go to the Bywater Brew Pub. They have a non-alcoholic hazy IPA on tap."

"On tap? Wow, that's unusual," said Jules.

"My thoughts exactly. Let me check on Adam real quick and let him know we are going for a ride."

Rick knocked on Adam's door and he answered right away.

"Hey Adam. Jules and I are going for a little bike ride. If you hear anything coming from our room, it's probably Chief, my cockatoo."

"You have a cockatoo?"

"Yeah, come over and meet him. Maybe he'll cheer you up. He's pretty sweet."

Adam followed Rick over to his room and his eyes lit up when he saw Chief.

"Oh, my goodness, he's so cute. Can I pet him?"

"Sure, just go slow. He's pretty chill," said Rick.

Adam reached up and petted Chief on the head. He cooed a little and seemed comfortable with Adam. Within minutes, Chief reached for him with his little foot. Adam stuck his hand out, and Chief stepped up on it. Adam pulled Chief to his chest, and they bonded immediately.

"So, he just stays on this perch when y'all are gone? He doesn't get lonely?"

"Yeah, he keeps himself busy with those tongue depressors. If you want, I can push him over to your room while we ride, so you can get to know each other."

"I'd like that a lot," replied Adam.

Rick grabbed a bag of grapes and the tongue depressors and pushed the PVC perch over to Adam's room. Adam walked behind Rick with Chief still snuggled up to his chest.

"Y'all have fun. We'll be back in a couple of hours. Call me if you need anything."

"We'll be fine, Rick. Have a good ride."

Rick and Jules unlocked their new bikes from the bike rack in the parking garage and pushed them up the street to Canal Street, heading toward the river. When they got to the trailhead, they rode leisurely. Jules pedaled slowly as he took in all the sights that the trail by the river had to offer. Street vendors hawked New Orleans memorabilia alongside palm readers who had set up card tables to tell strangers their fortunes or read Tarot cards.

Rick thought about Paul as he pedaled. It was a tragedy, and if Adam was innocent, he was determined to prove it. Rick had his GPS set for Bywater Brew Pub, which was running alongside his MapMyFitness app. When they reached the center of Crescent Park, they took a left and crossed over on the Rusty Rainbow Bridge to Piety Street, then made another left onto Royal and rode up a few more blocks. The unassuming corrugated aluminum building was painted red with yellow window frames. They locked the bikes to the bike rack on Royal Street, positioned between two trees.

The brewpub had a spacious, open area typical of many brewpubs, with several high-top tables and a merchandise section. As they entered, a local girl in the corner was playing cover tunes on her guitar. Rick ordered two of their non-alcoholic drafts while Jules found a table where they could sit.

"This is nice," said Rick.

"I know. I love the vibe of this place."

"No, not the place. Us. I love that we can get some exercise on the bikes and socialize without the need for alcohol. I don't miss it."

"Me either. You hardly ever use those BuzzDrops either anymore," said Jules.

"I have to be in the right state of mind to get out of my mind. Ha-ha. Understand?"

"Yeah, I get it."

They had a couple more of the drafts, tipped the performer, and walked back to their bikes.

"You hungry?" asked Rick.

"Peckish."

They rode back up Montegut Street to Chartres Street and stumbled into this little place called BABs, which stood for Bywater American Bistro. Attached to the restaurant in the courtyard was an area known as Yurt Village. They had set up several small yurts, which were uniquely shaped teepee-style tents featuring two-top tables inside.

"Odios mio! Can we grab a snack in one of those?" asked Jules.

When she said 'Oh my God' in Spanish, Rick knew she was excited. So, he found the hostess and tipped her twenty bucks to let them sit there and just have a couple of appetizers. The yurts were normally reserved for full dinners, but it was early, so she didn't mind. They sat inside one of the yurts as a waitress brought out a menu. Rick ordered a warm olive plate and some blackened octopus. After they nibbled on the starters, Rick asked Jules if she wanted to close the yurt curtain and make out.

"No, silly," she said as she playfully slapped him. "I want people to watch. Leave them open."

She gave Rick a long kiss. She was joking about making out, though, and Rick laughed. He paid the bill and left a generous tip. They got back on their bikes and made their way to the Crescent Trail, heading for the hotel. Once they arrived, Rick locked up the bikes and they went up to their hotel room.

CHAPTER
SEVEN

H is phone started going off. It was several texts from Possum with the last one all in caps.

CALL ME!

They got up from their room, and Jules said she'd check on Adam and Chief while Rick called Possum.

"Rick, I went down to the morgue to see if there had been any developments. I had to tell them I was his cousin to get in. They thawed out Paul and carved on his chest were the words, NOW YOUR THE MEAT. Whoever did it misspelled 'you're' but the message was clear."

"That's sick. I spoke to the detective, and they are still waiting on forensics. However, they found a duffel bag in one of the dumpsters behind the hotel containing a stainless-steel cable with wooden dowels. It was used as a ligature and is covered in blood. In the other dumpster, they found a bunch of rolled-up clothes. The coroner believes the cause of death was asphyxiation caused by a ligature. If that bag belongs to Adam, I think they will have enough to charge him. The detective stated that, based on this information and the results of the DNA blood test from the forensics lab, they will most likely convene a grand jury and indict him. If they do, they could seek the death penalty because of the heinous nature of the crime," said Possum.

"Fuck, that doesn't look good. I'm gonna talk to Adam. What did the duffel bag look like?" asked Rick.

"It was a camo Under Armor duffel. They swabbed the bag for DNA as well. If it's his, I'm sure they are going to charge him. I'm afraid."

"Do you think he did it? My gut tells me no."

"We don't know him that well. He seemed like a nice, respectful guy on the set, but anything is possible."

"Okay, thanks, Possum. I'm gonna go talk to him. I'll get back to you later," said Rick. He called Adam's lawyer before going to talk to Adam.

"Hi Mr. Thomas. It's Rick Waters. Did you hear from the detectives yet?"

"Oh, hi Rick. I just got off the phone with Detective Jones. He told me everything. Are you up to speed?"

"Yeah, pretty sick. Do you think they are going to charge Adam?"

"I do. Those detectives have blinders on, and they are focused on Adam. It's typical. If they do charge him, the judge will probably set bail for a million dollars. I guess he'll have to wait in jail until trial."

"Don't count on it. My partner at my private detective

agency has access to a vast amount of resources. If I ask him to pay the bail bond, he will. I'm sure the judge will confiscate Adam's passport since he might think he'd be a flight risk. Let me ask you a question. Do you think Adam would be stupid enough to dispose of the murder weapon in the dumpster behind his own hotel? It doesn't add up."

"You think he's being framed?"

"One hundred percent!" replied Rick.

"By who?"

"Jealous ex, maybe? It's either someone who knows him or someone who is aware of his relationship with Paul and knows that the police always look at the spouse or domestic partner first. I'm gonna go talk to Adam now. I'll keep you posted."

"Ditto, Rick. Bye for now."

Rick walked over to Paul's old room, where Adam was now staying. Jules was talking to him and playing with Chief, with the door held open by the swing bar door guard.

"Knock, knock," said Rick.

"Come in, Rick," replied Adam.

"I see you and Chief are still getting along."

"He's amazing. Thanks for letting me hang out with him."

"No worries. Listen. I have a question for you. Can you describe your duffel bag?" asked Rick.

"Nothing special. It's a camo Under Armor bag. I don't need a big bag because I roll my clothes when I pack. Why?"

"I was afraid you were gonna say that. They found your duffel in a dumpster behind the hotel. It had a steel cable ligature inside it with blood on it. It's the murder weapon. I think they are gonna charge you with Paul's murder. I'm sorry."

"Oh my God. This can't be happening to me. I didn't do anything! I swear. None of this makes sense. Are they even looking at anyone else?"

"Probably not. As usual, they will want to wrap this case up as fast as possible. They have blinders on for you," said Rick.

"Am I going to jail?" asked Adam.

"Probably. But don't worry. We will bail you out as soon as possible. I'm gonna talk to my partner about the bail money. Did they take a blood test or urine test from you at the station?"

"They did draw my blood."

"Okay. I'm gonna head down to the station. Just sit tight. You can keep Chief in the room with you if you'd like," said Rick.

"Jules, you want to go with me?"

"Sure, let me grab my purse."

Rick and Jules headed down to the sheriff's department and found out that they had sent Adam's blood to the Louisiana State Police Crime Lab on Lakeshore Drive, so they drove over there. After speaking to a woman at the front desk, they hit a brick wall. They wouldn't answer any of Rick's questions and certainly weren't giving him any information about the results.

"I have an idea. Let's go pick up Adam. Can you text him on my phone while I drive and tell him we are on the way and to meet us in front of the hotel?" asked Rick.

"Sure."

When they arrived, Adam was sitting on the curb outside of the hotel.

"Hey, Rick. What's up? I left Chief on the perch in my room with the TV on. Will he be okay?"

"He'll be fine."

"Where are we going?"

"LabCorp. You said you never do hard drugs, right?"

"Nope, never. I'm all natural and never took steroids either."

"Good. I have a theory. Bear with me," said Rick.

They pulled up to LabCorp, and Rick spoke with one of the employees. They brought Adam to the back, drew his blood, and had him pee into a cup. He came back to the lobby a few minutes later.

"I'm done. Not sure why I did that, but I'm done," said Adam.

"I think you are being framed. I had the lab do a drug screen on you and specifically look for Rohypnol."

"Rohypnol? What's that?" asked Adam.

"It's commonly known as the date rape drug. It and other drugs like it can cause blackouts and total memory loss. I have a theory, but proving it won't be easy. You said you had a Yeti cup with you when you were working out, right?"

"Yeah, why?"

"Was there anyone else in the gym with you last night? Also, did you ever have the Yeti cup out of your sight?"

Adam thought for a minute.

"As a matter of fact, there was a guy in there. I was using the bench press, and my cup was sitting on the floor beside me. After I finished my last set on the bench press, I stepped into the bathroom to take a pee. I heard the door from the pool open to the gym, and then the treadmill started up. I cracked open the door to the bathroom to see who it was, thinking it might be Paul. He said he might join me in the gym once he was finished filming that day at the set. I saw that someone straddling the treadmill as it was running. He was wearing headphones and had his phone out, and it appeared as though he was scrolling on it for something to listen to before he stepped on the treadmill belt. I didn't think anything of it. I never saw his face. When I returned, he was gone, but my cup was still in the same spot where I left it."

"Bingo. The guy wearing the hoodie is the killer."

"Huh?"

"I think when you went to the bathroom, he put something in your recovery drink. You said the last thing you remember was finishing your kettlebell workout, right? How long after you returned from the bathroom did you do those?"

"It was right after I returned from the bathroom. I did three sets of kettlebell swings and three sets of kettlebell windmills. The windmills are the last thing I remember from the entire night."

"How long did those two sets take?" asked Rick.

"I'd say about fifteen minutes or so."

"I knew it," said Rick as he slapped his knee. Those kind of drugs takes effect about fifteen to twenty minutes after ingesting, according to the website drugrehab.com. I'd bet you a million dollars there's one of them in your system. We'll know soon enough."

They returned to the hotel and called it a night. Possum texted Rick to inform him that the sheriff's department had released the set and that they could resume filming in the morning. Rick allowed Chief to spend the night with Adam for company. Jules ordered room service, and they were in bed by 10:00 p.m. Possum set an 8:00 a.m. call time. It would be the first day Jules would get to play a voodoo queen.

"Goodnight, baby," said Rick as he kissed Jules on the forehead.

"I love you."

"Ditto Mrs. Waters."

Jules smiled and turned off the light on her nightstand. Rick put on his sleep mask with headphones and selected a podcast about UFOs on Spotify to help him sleep. He was out within fifteen minutes.

Rick and Jules arrived at 7:30 a.m. at the set. The production company was already scurrying around like a colony of ants. Possum had borrowed a cool altar from a real practicing voodoo princess for Jules to use on the set. He also paid the woman to consult for the film. He wanted it to be as authentic as possible. She brought several pieces of voodoo paraphernalia and ritual items, including chicken feet, black candles, voodoo dolls, gris gris bags, and more.

Rick had downloaded the ebook, *A New Orleans Voudou Priestess: The Legend and Reality of Marie Laveau,* on Jules'

Kindle for her to read, and she had already read most of it. She was taking this character seriously.

Rick stepped into the editing trailer where Possum was posted up.

"How long have you been editing?" asked Rick.

"I did it until about 2:15 a.m. this morning, slept for a few hours, and got back up at six and started again."

"How's it going?"

"It's going well. I'm about three-quarters of the way through it, and I'm getting better as I go. I talked to Gary, and he's gonna pay for a sound guy to come in and tweak the audio. He's also agreed to pay for a music supervisor to choose the perfect songs for all the scenes. It's gonna be fantastic when it's done," said Possum.

"That's great. I'm eager to watch it. When are we shooting Jules' first scene?"

"Soon. I ordered a fog machine, and it should be here shortly. As soon as it arrives, I'll do an ambient light test, and we can begin. I wanna get a couple of shots done while the sun is still low on the horizon. I'm stoked that it's overcast today."

"Awesome. Okay, I'm gonna go check on Jules and see how her makeup is coming along."

"Oh, I had to hire a new assistant director. He's a local. His name is Antoine. You need to meet him. He's quite a character. Go introduce yourself. He's in the craft services tent."

"Will do."

Rick went over to Jule's trailer, where Richard had Jules looking beautiful, if not mysterious and a bit scary at the same time. Her wardrobe and makeup were perfect. After giving them the thumbs up, he walked over to the craft service tent and found Antoine. He was about six feet five with a tight afro and extremely lean. His voice bellowed when he spoke.

"Hi Antoine, I'm Rick. One of the actors, well, sort of, and also Possum's partner in the film. My wife Jules is playing the voodoo queen."

"So, Rick, you're sort of an actor? Well, I'm sort of black. Believe in yourself, man. There's nothing you can't accomplish in life if you believe in yourself. Now, I want you to introduce yourself again, but this time with conviction."

"Uh, okay. Hi. I'm Rick Waters, I'm one of the actors in this movie," said Rick.

"Yes, yes, yes!" said Antoine as he jumped up and down. "Now, that's an introduction and I believe deep down that you are an actor."

Antoine was incredibly eccentric and positive, and Rick liked him right away. Rick poured himself a cup of coffee and reviewed the day's script. It was all Jules. Rick would watch and give her moral support. A truck pulled up and unloaded a fog machine. The crew placed it beside the clearing down by the water, where they had scouted for the altar. They plugged it in and cranked it up. It pumped out an immense amount of fog that floated just above the water. Possum came out and checked the lighting, called for Jules and the man playing the original dead person she would bring back to life to position. He lay on the altar, and Jules stood behind him. After tweaking the lights a little, Antoine called for quiet on the set.

"And action," said Possum.

Jules began to speak in tongues as her eyes rolled back in her head. She was born for this role. She started speaking Patois French, which wasn't in the script, but she was improvising. Possum let the camera continue to roll.

"Ramène cet homme d'entre les morts," she said as she waved one of the chicken feet over his head.

She got fire in her eyes and screamed, "Laissez-le vivre!"

Rick understood that line. It meant, let him live.

The man's finger twitched, and he began to shake slightly. His eyes opened as he sat up on the altar. Jules blew some powder in his face, and he slowly spun around, walking past the camera with a staggered limp.

"Cut!" yelled Possum. "That was perfect. Let's do it one more time for safety before the sun comes up anymore."

Jules and the man returned to their positions and performed the scene again. It was nearly identical, if not slightly better. For the rest of the day, Possum filmed B-roll of zombies emerging from the water in the bayou and climbing out of the mausoleums constructed by the set designer. Antoine had a great idea to film in the graveyard where Marie Laveau's mausoleum was located. He knew exactly which one it was, and it had three x's on it.

"We're gonna need a filming permit for that," said Possum.

"Let's beg for forgiveness instead of asking for permission. Besides, I know a guy at the permit office. He's as crooked as a barrel of catfish hooks. If you grease him, he'll write you a permit after the fact. Trust me," said Antoine.

That Antoine is something else, Rick thought.

After they finished the day's B-roll, they took a small crew and two cameras out to St. Louis Cemetery No. 1. Antoine tipped the gate guard, and they went inside. The sun was setting, and the light was perfect. Possum had written a small scene on the way for Jules to act out. She would summon the power of Marie Laveau and use it to bring back the dead. She used Google Translate to split it half and half between English and French.

The shots went perfectly, and they wrapped up for the night. Possum mentioned that he was returning to the refuge to continue editing the movie they filmed in Egypt. Rick tried to talk Possum into taking a break, but he was hell bent on finishing the first edits of the film. Rick knew Craft Services was already shut down at the set, so he would surprise Possum and have a pizza delivered to him from Slidell. Sometimes when Possum would get caught up in a project, he'd forget to eat. Rick was just taking care of his good old friend. Rick and Jules had a long day and decided to go back to the hotel and relax instead of going out to dinner. They stopped off at Adam's room, and he was content to hang out with Chief again. Rick was beginning to regret sending Chief over there to keep him company and was missing him.

As tired as they were, they felt it would be good for them to work out at the gym a little and get into the sauna before calling it a night. Since Adam had been cooped up in his room all day and was a personal trainer, Rick thought it would kill two birds with one stone if he could get Adam to come work out with them. It would get Adam out of his room, and Rick could learn a thing or two. He had heard Joe Rogan on his podcast talk about how good kettlebell workouts could be and wanted to give them a try. He remembered Adam talking about doing a set of kettlebell workouts and figured he'd know what he was doing. So, they changed into their gym attire and Rick knocked on his door.

"Hi Adam. Jules and I are heading down to the gym. I was wondering if you'd like to join us and maybe give me a pointer or two about those kettlebell workouts."

"I'd love to. It's the least I can do. You have been so kind to me. While I'm a guest in this hotel, consider me your own personal trainer. Free of charge, of course. Let me change real quick, and I'll meet you both down there," said Adam.

"Great. I'll head down and do some stretching until you arrive," said Rick.

"You read my mind. See ya shortly."

Rick had an ulterior motive besides learning kettlebell exercises. He wanted to get to know Adam better and assess him a little more. There was still a small sliver of a chance that he was the killer, and if Rick was going to continue to support him, he wanted to resolve that issue or walk away.

Rick sat on a padded bench by the elliptical machine, crossing his legs and pulling up on his knee. He always did that because it helped with sciatica. He would first pull his knee up for thirty seconds, then push against it for thirty seconds, and then switch legs. Rick had always been tight for as long as he could remember. He could barely touch his toes, and it bothered him. He was jealous of Jules; she was limber as spaghetti. Not only could she touch her toes, but she could also flatten out completely and put her head between her knees and even a little behind them. It amazed him.

"How the hell do you do that?" asked Rick.

"Don't know. Always have been able to," replied Jules.

"You're blessed."

Rick moaned and groaned as he stretched. He had sprinter legs, and it hurt every time he stretched. He hated it more than almost anything but forced himself to do it. He was halfway through his hamstring stretches when Adam entered the gym.

"Rick, hold on. I can help you with that. Some friends of mine from Finland have discovered that one of the reasons a person is tight is not just because of the muscles, but first, it's because of tightness in the nervous system. You can stretch your muscles all you want, but if you don't attack the root cause, they will just spring back into tightness. I highly recommend that you sign up for their course at movement-world.com. You can then follow along daily on your own and stretch out those pesky nerves. Until then, let me show you."

Rick had never heard of such a thing and was a bit skeptical, but the more Adam explained, the more he accepted it. So much so that he added the website to his Notes app on his iPhone and vowed to sign up.

"So, the way the nerve stretches work is that you divide your body into two sections: the upper half and the lower half. You can alternate days or do them both in one day. I prefer to alternate because of time constraints. Since I can see you are so tight, you should do both for a while, then alternate after a week or two. We're gonna start with your neck. Make a fist with your left hand and place it under your right armpit, then grab your left elbow with your right hand. See how your right shoulder is now higher than your left shoulder? That shortens the muscle on that side. Now while in that position, bend your neck to the left until you feel the stretch. Do that six times, then switch sides and do the same thing."

Rick did one side and then the other.

"You feel that?" asked Adam. Do it on each side three times, and then we will move on."

Rick did three sets on each side. Jules was following along too.

Next, we will do the archery stretch. Point your arms forward away from your chest horizontally and cup your hands together. Now pull your left hand back as if pulling the string of a bow and arrow, keeping your head forward while letting your back turn toward the pulled-back arm. Keep your hips and pelvis straight. "Feel that?" asked Adam.

When Rick did the opposite side, his back cracked. It felt good.

"Wow, that's amazing," said Rick.

"Okay, now do three sets."

Rick and Jules both completed the exercises, and then they moved on to the third one. Adam was incredibly knowledgeable and guided them through it slowly and confidently. Once they finished all the nervous system stretches, he began to demonstrate the kettlebell exercises to Rick. Rick chose a twenty-pound kettlebell, while Jules used a ten-pounder. Adam went through each exercise thoroughly, and Rick took notes on his iPhone. Between exercises, Rick took the time to ask Adam questions about his relationship with Paul, as well as about his upbringing and academic studies. Adam provided no information that raised red flags for Rick.

As it was a closed set and Paul was responsible for keeping track of all the names of the extras and crew, he maintained a notebook with each person's details. The problem was that the notebook was missing. He had a feeling that the real killer was listed in that notebook, but without it, he had no idea who might have stopped coming after Paul had been murdered. If Rick could find that notebook, it would greatly aid in solving who Paul's murderer was. Adam continued to demonstrate each exercise and gave Rick time to take notes in his Notes app on his iPhone.

"You remind me of Paul," said Adam.

"How's that?"

"Paul always used that app. Whenever he received a business card from someone, he would take a photo of it, copy it to the Notes app, and throw away the card. He said he always misplaced cards, and if he put them on his phone and into iCloud, he'd never lose them. A lightbulb went off in Rick's head and he thought it might be possible that Paul had added the list from his notebook to his phone, which would also be on his iCloud. Since his phone was missing, maybe it was backed up to the iCloud.

"Do you happen to know what email address and password Paul used for his iCloud?" asked Rick.

"I assume he used his main email which was paulrstras berg1976@gmail.com. I don't know what his password is but he once told me he used the password Germany12!!. I remember that because he told me he was frustrated because one of the apps he used made him add special characters to his old password Germany12."

"Thanks Adam. It's too bad the notebook and his iPhone

are missing. It could help your case. I'll have Possum do some research on the iCloud. He's a bit of a hacker," said Rick.

After the workout, Rick stretched again, and then he and Jules headed up to the room. Out of curiosity, he opened his MacBook and signed out of his iCloud. He signed back in using Paul's email address and tried the password Adam had given him, but it didn't work. He tried another one similar, and it didn't work, so he texted Possum all the info and let him try to hack into it. He ordered room service, and before it arrived, Possum texted him back.

I'm in. It's Germany1234!!

You are amazing!

After a quick shower, Rick logged into Paul's iCloud account and downloaded all the notes to his MacBook. He discovered numerous notes on lighting, wardrobe, and locations for the movie. As he scrolled down, he came across multiple photos of business cards. He decided to try a search and typed "extras" in the search bar. A photo appeared, and Rick opened it. It contained pages from the notebook listing all the extras, actors, and crew from the movie. Each page was dated and comprehensive. Rick took some hotel stationery and began writing down the names of the extras and crew for each day. As he moved to the next day, if someone didn't appear on set, he would mark the date next to their name.

It was tedious, and because extras sometimes worked only one day and never returned, or worked a day, then left and came back, it would take a long time to identify potential suspects. After an hour, he compiled ten names of individuals who were on set the night Paul was murdered and then never returned. He planned to keep track of the names and start researching each one since the film was still in progress, with many more scenes involving the extras. Rick ate dinner and continued to work on the list. He was starting to yawn and Jules had already gone to bed, so he snuggled up next to her and fell asleep within minutes.

CHAPTER
EIGHT

Rick was awakened by a text from Todd Thomas, Adam's lawyer.

Call me immediately.

Rick wiped his eyes and called Todd.

"What's up, Todd?"

"Rick, I just found out that the forensic results came back, and the blood found in Adam's hotel belonged to Paul. I'm sure they will be assembling a grand jury and indicting him. It doesn't look good. I know Adam believes he was framed, and I'm beginning to think so too. It all seems so tidy. I wanted you to know because if he is indicted, as I said before, the judge will set a high bail, if he sets one at all. It's possible he may not allow bail. I will keep you updated, but please let your partner know that he might have to pay a significant bond. I will urge the judge for a lower bond, but it's ultimately his decision."

"Thanks Todd. Do you want me to tell Adam, or will you call him?"

"That may be something better to do in person. Let's wait until I find out if they indict him. You will be the first to know," said Todd.

"Okay, thanks Todd. Talk to you soon."

Rick checked his email, and he still hadn't received the results from Adam's test at LabCorp. Possum had set a noon call time for a daytime scene on Bourbon Street. It would be a funny scene where zombies would be stumbling down Bourbon Street during Mardi Gras, and because of the way they staggered when they walked, they would resemble drunk people walking down Bourbon Street. Rick wanted to arrive early and get all the extras' names on the list, so he could cross-check it with the night Paul was murdered. He made a pot of coffee and ordered some croissants and fruit from room service. Jules was already in the bathroom getting ready for the day when breakfast arrived. They ate together on the balcony and discussed the funny scene planned for the day.

"Who wrote that scene?" asked Jules.

"I'm not sure. Probably Possum. I know he is a huge fan of Zombieland, which is full of humor. The scene has Possum's fingerprints all over it," said Rick.

"I love that movie," replied Jules.

"Yeah, me too. You ready to head to the Quarter? We can take our bikes if you want to."

"Great idea."

Rick and Jules checked on Adam and Chief, and they were both doing great. Rick didn't mention anything to

Adam about what Todd had told him. There was no reason to make him worry until they had more info. Rick and Jules unlocked their bikes and pedaled down Canal Street, taking a right on Royal Street up to Bourbon Street. Security was tight, involving both the private security team hired by the film producer and local New Orleans police. Rick was glad that even he and Jules were required to show IDs to get on the set. The head of security had taken charge of the master list of the extras and crew and after speaking to him, he let Rick photograph a copy of the list once everyone had arrived for the shoot. He quickly went down the list and made note of any of the ten names that had been MIA since the murder.

The new assistant director called for quiet on the set, and Possum called action to start the first scene. He had the zombies walk in the same direction up Bourbon Street. Some of them had beads hanging from their necks. He even set up a *Big Ass Beer* street cart, and a couple of the zombies picked up beers and walked with them, arms extended in front of them. The scene was incredibly funny. After shooting several takes, the next scene would be filmed at the world-famous Pat O'Brien's Bar. It would involve a group of college kids doing a zombie crawl bar hop, and a real zombie stumbles into the bar. The group of college students revels in how good his costume is, not knowing yet that there has been a real zombie outbreak, as they toast the zombie with hurricanes and compliment the zombie on the realism of his costume. One of the students gets close to him to pat him on the back, and the zombie bites a huge chunk out of the student's neck, causing the rest of the students to reel in horror. It was a brilliant scene.

After calling for action, the cameraman filmed the students at a table partying with several rounds of hurricanes. A second cameraman did an over-the-shoulder shot of the real zombie stumbling into the bar. Rick and Jules stood off camera and watched.

"Woohoo! Let's get another round!" exclaimed one of the college frat guys.

A few minutes later, a waitress brought out a large tray of hurricanes, and the drunk students flirted with her.

"Look at that zombie costume. It fucking rocks!" said one of the college students as a particularly gruesome real zombie stumbled into the bar.

"That's the most realistic makeup I've ever seen. Take my picture with him," said another student as he walked up to the real zombie, patted him on the back, gave him props, and put his arm around him.

As another student took out their phone to snap a quick photo, the real zombie turned its head and bit the student on the neck, causing blood to spurt all over the zombie. Blood pulsed and gushed from the student's neck. Richard, the makeup designer, created such a realistic wound that, even while watching it live, it looked real. All the other students thought for a second it was a gag until their friend fell to the ground, and the real zombie knelt down to rip out his guts and eat them. The students screamed with looks of horror and ran out of the bar, only to be attacked by zombies in the street. This scene was particularly tough to shoot because it involved two separate camera teams and wardrobe changes due to all the fake blood. Richard also had to clean up the student the zombie ate and redo his blood packs and fake wounds.

It took almost two hours between takes, and Possum made an executive decision to limit it to just two takes. He had a budget to consider, and the first take was so good that it would be hard to beat.

"Possum, we're gonna head back to the hotel since we're not in any scenes. I want to start researching some of the names on the extras list."

"No worries, Amigo. Oh, and thanks for the pizza last night. It hit the spot."

"My pleasure, buddy. I would hate for you to starve to death."

"No chance of that. Keep me posted on what you find out. If you need any help, please don't hesitate to let me know. After I wrap here for the day, I'm gonna head back to the set at the refuge and do some more editing," said Possum.

"Sounds good."

When Rick and Jules pulled up to the hotel, five police cars and a SWAT van sat out front of the hotel.

"Oh shit!" exclaimed Rick.

"What happened?" asked Jules.

"I think they arrested Adam for Paul's murder."

Rick had Jules hold his bicycle, and he ran into the lobby. He found the officer in charge, and while he wouldn't give Rick Adam's name, he did tell him they were at the hotel to execute a warrant for someone's arrest. Within minutes, police escorted Adam through the center of the lobby.

"Don't say anything, Adam. I'll call your lawyer!" yelled Rick.

"Thanks, Chief is still in the room. He's upset," said Adam.

Rick spoke to a deputy and explained that it was his cockatoo in the room. Once Adam had been placed into a squad car and moved to the detention center, the SWAT team allowed Rick into Adam's room to retrieve Chief. Jules had locked up the bikes in the parking garage and joined Rick. Chief was sitting on the perch, shivering. Rick picked him up and brought him to his chest. Chief continued to shiver, and Rick petted him as Jules spoke softly to him. He eventually calmed down, so Jules carried his perch to their room, and Rick followed her.

"Damn, he looks traumatized. Those damn cops always overdo it. Adam would've turned himself in if they had just told us ahead of time," said Rick.

"I know, but they love to flash their guns and play soldier. It pisses me off!" exclaimed Jules.

Rick's phone started going off. It was Todd.

"They got him, Todd. They came in with automatic weapons and took him away. Ridiculous."

"I just heard. They convened the grand jury and indicted him faster than I thought possible. There is a hearing scheduled for the morning, during which the judge may set the bond amount. Can you and your partner attend the hearing?" asked Todd.

"Yeah, we'll be there. Just text me the time."

"They have a ton of evidence against Adam. They tested the murder weapon in the duffle bag and found both Adam's and Paul's DNA on it. It looks real bad. Did you get the results of Adam's drug test yet?" asked Todd.

"Not yet. I'm gonna call them after I get off with you."

"Okay, Rick. Keep me posted."

"Will do."

Rick called LabCorp, and they informed him that they would email the results by the end of the day. Rick ended the call and began a NEXIS research of the ten names that never showed back up to the set after the night of Paul's murder; all but three still had not returned to the set. So, he focused on those. None of the extras had criminal records, but one had been arrested but not convicted of criminal trespassing and assault. The case was dropped when the victim failed to appear at the hearing. Rick focused on that extra. His name was Jason Bagley. Rick did a search for him on social media and found out he was a far-left nut job who had attended many protests, mostly environmental. Rick went into his photos and found one of himself that was taken at the Animal Rights Protest Day in 2015.

"Bingo!" exclaimed Rick.

He looked through Jason's photos and found one of him smiling. He was missing a couple of teeth on the right side of his mouth. Rick remembered the crime scene photos of the bite taken out of Paul's face and that the bitemark was jagged. He immediately called Todd.

"Hey Todd. Can you send me a copy of Paul's autopsy photos?"

"Sure, why?"

"I'll explain later."

A few moments went by, and Rick's phone vibrated; all

the photos arrived from the autopsy. He zoomed into the one of the bite mark on Paul's face, and it was clear that whoever bit him was missing a tooth. Jason Bagley had just moved from unknown extra to potential suspect. Rick had to find him and speak to him. His last place of residence was Gretna, Louisiana.

He called Todd back.

"Did they do a cast of the bite mark on Paul's face?"

"I think they did. The autopsy is complete, by the way. I just got off the phone with the coroner. They have ruled the cause of death as murder and the manner of death as strangulation by ligature," said Todd.

"Did they test the bite for DNA? I assume they did. Let me check my notes."

A few moments went by, and Rick could hear Todd shuffling through some papers.

"I can't find that. Let me call the ME and get back to you."

"Alright, Todd. It's important. I think I may have an alternate suspect for you."

Rick opened a Diet Coke while he waited for Todd to return his call. After about ten minutes, Rick's phone rang.

"Talk to me," said Rick.

"They did not do a DNA test on the bite mark."

"Why the hell not?"

"I'm not sure. The ME just skipped that."

"Well, let's have it tested then," said Rick.

There was a long pause on the phone.

"I have bad news. The body was released to the family

after the autopsy was finished and he was cremated. The ashes were flown to Germany this morning."

"You've got to be fucking kidding me!"

"I wish I was. The parents had every right to do that though."

"We still have the cast, though, right?"

"Yeah. We do."

"Okay. I'm gonna take a ride. I'll talk to you soon."

Rick ended the call and got Jules' attention.

"Hey Jules. Wanna take a ride with me? Chief can come with us."

"Sure. Let me grab my shoes. Where are we going?"

"Gretna."

Rick crossed over the mighty Mississippi on the Crescent City Connection bridge. Jules peered out over the bridge at the muddy brown water and all the tugboats and barges with Chief sitting on her lap. Once they arrived in Greta, Rick exited onto Stumph Boulevard and took a right onto Kepler Street. He found the address where Jason lived, and when he pulled up, he saw crime scene tape around the house. He pulled past it and parked. He had Jules wait in the car with Chief and he walked up to the house. He saw a neighbor mowing his grass, caught his attention, and asked him what had happened.

"He overdosed," said the man.

"Oh, that's too bad. I met Jason on a movie shoot when I was working as an extra. He told me if I was ever in town, to look him up. What a shame. When did he OD?" asked Rick.

"It was on the 5th."

That was the day after Paul was murdered, thought Rick.

Rick was about to walk away when the neighbor said,

"We were all shocked. I've lived next to Jason for years. He was a little eccentric and an animal lover. He attended numerous animal rights protests and regularly donated money. A real stand-up guy. I never, ever once saw him do drugs. Hell, he wouldn't even smoke pot. We played cards together. The only thing I ever saw him do was drink beer. He loved his beer. All styles of beer, but he was no drug addict. I think he even went to Oktoberfest. Plus, he was terrified of needles. I tried to get him to give blood one day when the Big Red Bus was in our neighborhood, and he said he stayed as far away from needles as possible. I still can't believe he overdosed on heroin. Makes no sense. We loved him. No one cared that he was gay."

Rick thanked the man and returned to the Jeep.

"What happened?" asked Jules.

"The neighbor said he overdosed. The funny thing is, he was never a drug user and was scared of needles. He said Jason overdosed on heroin. I need to see his toxicology report. Let's go down to the lab and see what we can find out."

Rick pulled up to the coroner's office and stepped inside.

"Hi, I'm trying to find the toxicology report for a Jason Bagley of Gretna. Can you help me?" asked Rick.

"You need to go to the Louisiana Department of Health on Poydras Street and file a public records request. There is a small fee."

"Thanks," said Rick.

"Did you get it?" asked Jules.

"Nope, more hoops to jump through."

Rick parked at the Louisiana Department of Health, filled out the form, and paid the fee. A few minutes later, the woman behind the window brought out the printed report from Jason's toxicology report. His cause of death was ruled as acute toxicity from diacetylmorphine. He had to look that up on Google to find out that diacetylmorphine was the scientific name for heroin. He did some research and found out that Jason had already been buried. His body was laid to rest at Westlawn Memorial Park in Gretna. Rick needed to find Jason's next of kin. He had a gut feeling that Jason was murdered and didn't overdose. The only way to find out was to exhume his body and test for other poisons. For that, he'd need the family's permission. He did a quick search and found out his mother was still alive and lived in Greta not too far from where Jason lived.

"Jules, I'm gonna need your help. We have to speak to Jason's mother and talk her into letting us exhume his body. I don't think he overdosed."

"I'll do whatever you think will help," said Jules.

Rick crossed the bridge again and found Jason's mother's house. He parked on the street, and Jules placed Chief in the travel backpack in the Jeep. Rick and Jules walked up to the front door, and Rick rang the doorbell.

"Can I help you?" she said as she cracked open the door.

"Hi, Mrs. Bagley. My name is Rick Waters, and this is Jules. I'd like to discuss your son with you. First, let me tell you how sorry I am for your loss. Secondly, I don't think Jason overdosed. I believe he was murdered," said Rick.

"Murdered? I thought the same thing. I told the cops he

never would've overdosed. They wouldn't listen to me," she said as she took the latch off the door and opened it up.

"The only way we can know for sure is to exhume his body and do some more tests," said Rick.

"I don't know. We already put him to rest. I'm not comfortable with that."

"Mrs. Bagley. I know how hard it is when you lose someone close. Back in Colombia, I had some friends murdered by the cartel. I feel your pain. Don't you want the killer to be brought to justice? We can help," said Jules.

The woman thought for a few minutes.

"I'm upset that the cops treated him like a drug addict. He didn't do drugs. I know that for a fact. Okay, what do I have to do?" asked Mrs. Bagley.

"I will get the form for you to sign and take care of it for you. I will keep you in the loop. May I have your phone number?"

She stepped away from the door and brought Rick a piece of scrap paper with her number on it.

"Thank you, mister. You too miss," she said.

"No, thank you, Mrs. Bagley. We will do right by your son. I promise," said Rick.

She put her hand to her heart, and Rick and Jules returned to the Jeep.

"I could feel her pain," said Jules.

"Me too."

CHAPTER
NINE

Rick, Jules, and Gary sat in the courtroom. The judge walked in, and the bailiff asked everyone to stand as he announced the arrival of the Honorable Judge Matthew Morgan.

"Good morning, everybody. Please, be seated," said the judge.

"Your Honor, the State requests that the defendant be remanded without bail," said the black female prosecutor. "Mr. Olsen is charged with murder in the first degree in connection with the brutal slaying of Paul Strasberg, a crime that was premeditated, violent, and calculated. He poses an extreme flight risk and a danger to the community,"

Judge Morgan nodded slowly, considering. "Thank you, Ms. Jackson.

"Defense counsel?" asked the judge.

Olsen's attorney, Todd Thomas, rose. "Your Honor, while

we understand the seriousness of the charges, Mr. Olsen has no prior criminal record, and is willing to surrender his passport. We ask that bail be set at a reasonable amount so that he may prepare his defense from outside of detention."

A long moment passed. Judge Morgan leaned back in his chair and folded his hands.

"This court has reviewed the evidence presented and taken into account the gravity of the charge—murder in the first degree, with credible allegations of premeditation and intent. The victim, Paul Strasberg, suffered a violent and deliberate death. Might I add, quite gruesome. While the defendant has no prior record, the nature of this alleged crime and the potential sentence it carries raise substantial concern about flight risk."

He paused, then continued in a firm, measured tone:

"Bail is hereby set in the amount of five million dollars. Mr. Olsen shall be required to surrender his passport immediately. Should he post bail, he will be placed under electronic monitoring and home confinement pending trial."

"Thank you, your Honor. I ask that once bail has been posted, Mr. Olsen be allowed to serve house arrest under the remand of Mr. Rick Waters at the Windsor Court Hotel since Mr. Olsen is from Germany and has no house or family in the country."

The judge looked up again, his voice firmer now. "However, the court has also reviewed the affidavit submitted by Mr. Rick Waters. Given Mr. Waters' willingness to assume full responsibility for Mr. Olsen's whereabouts and conduct, I am granting the request to allow Mr. Waters to act as a custodian. If bail is posted, and only under that condition,

Mr. Olsen may reside under Mr. Waters' direct supervision in lieu of house arrest—provided all terms of monitoring remain in effect."

There was a pause as the weight of the decision settled over the room. A murmur passed through the courtroom. Rick, sat quietly beside Gary and Jules in the second row, gave a subtle nod. Judge Morgan struck the gavel once.

"Next matter on the docket."

Todd turned around and whispered to Gary as a deputy put handcuffs back on Adam and led him away.

"You know that's five hundred thousand dollars bail, right?"

"We got him covered," replied Gary.

"They may want additional collateral since it's such a high-profile case."

"I can put up my Prevost Tour Bus. It's valued at over two million," said Gary.

"That ought to do it. Go and see AAA Bail Bonds. Ask for Jack. I've had several clients use him. He's a good man," said Todd. "I'll let Adam know what's going on. Go now. The sooner the better."

Gary nodded and left the courtroom. Rick shared his new theory with Todd about Jason not overdosing and possibly being the killer.

"I don't know anymore. It's starting to feel like a conspiracy. I was certain Jason was the killer, but I think someone killed him. I'll know more once we exhume the body. Can you get a copy of his autopsy photos and send them to me?" asked Rick.

"Sure. I'll text them. Give me some time. I have to speak

to the ME in Greta. I can't pull any strings over there. I have to go through the same steps any lawyer would there," said Todd.

"I understand. Thanks."

Rick and Jules left the courthouse and started driving to Metairie. The Louisiana State Board of Embalmers and Funeral Directors was located there, and that was the only place to get the forms to have Jason's body exhumed. Luckily, it was a short drive. They picked up the forms, took them to Mrs. Bagley to sign, and returned them before closing. Once they were stamped, Rick drove to Westlawn Memorial Park in Gretna and gave the papers to the funeral director. He made the proper arrangements and called the ME in Gretna to bring the van. They wouldn't be able to do it until the next day, but that was pretty quick, Rick thought.

It was after 6:00 p.m. when Rick and Jules returned to the hotel. They fed Chief, and Jules looked online to find a place to eat that night. They wanted something simple and quick. She found a deli on Royal Street called Verti Marte that served muffalettas. They decided to walk over. It was a beautiful night, and they thought it would be nice to take a walk. After their muffalettas, they stopped at the French Market - Shops of the Colonnade. The actual French Market closed at 5:00 p.m., but some shops at the Colonnade stayed open later. Rick tried on a few hats from Chapel Hats and settled on a cloth crusher hat. He could never have enough hats, and this one was good for travel as it could be thrown in a suitcase and would easily spring back to its shape once removed. Jules bought some New Orleans memorabilia and a new colorful blouse. They leisurely strolled back to the hotel, taking in the sights along the way. Jules had a sweet tooth, so they stopped off at Café Du Monde and ordered a couple of beignets. As many times as Rick had eaten them over the years, he never got tired of them. It was a great outdoor spot to people-watch. Jules spotted a woman setting up a card table on the corner of Jackson Square.

"Can we get our Tarot Cards read, Rick? Please," said Jules.

Rick didn't believe in that bullshit but wanted to make Jules happy.

"Sure, why don't we have yours done. I don't need mine done."

"Oh, come on, let's both do it."

"On one condition. I'm getting some when we get back to the hotel."

"That's a given!"

They strolled over to Jackson Square just as the local woman sat down and lit all her candles.

"Ahh, newlyweds. You want your Tarot Cards read?" she asked.

"Yep, that's why we're here," replied Jules as she sat down on a folding chair.

The dark woman began flipping cards after Rick handed her a twenty-dollar bill. She first flipped the moon card.

"You are facing uncertain, hidden truths, and confusion. Der is an emotional fog surrounding you dat is making tings appear differently than dey truly are," said the woman.

Jules looked up at Rick with amazement in her eyes.

The woman then flipped over the tower card.

"Dis card represents sudden upheaval, crisis, revelation, destruction of false foundations. A twist of fate awaits you. Keep your eyes open and heart even more open."

The third card she revealed was the star.

"Ah, dis card means hope, healing, inspiration, and renewal. Der will be a reckoning on what you are working on."

She flipped a few more cards over on top of each other, then said it was time to draw one last card. Slowly, she picked up the corner and flipped it over. The candles flickered in the wind. It was the death card. Jule's eyes grew wide and she grabbed Rick's hand. The woman noticed Jule's eyes and her fear.

"Dis card doesn't always mean death. It can represent transformation, endings, and change. I need to flip one more bonus card to revel what de death card means."

She slowly flipped over the next card and they gasped. It was the Ten of Swords.

"I'm sorry. It does mean death, child. It represents loss and a period of intense pain and suffering," she said.

Jules gripped Rick's arm tightly and started to shiver. He wanted her to calm down, so he told the woman he wanted to be next.

"You don't understand, mista. Deez card were for you."

"Let's go, Jules. I've heard enough!"

Rick was upset that the woman scared Jules. She was easily frightened by silly things like that. He knew it was a bad idea for them to mess around with that crazy woman.

"Don't worry, Jules. She's a con. That stuff is total bullshit."

Jules was still shaking and no matter what Rick said, she was fearful. She was afraid someone would try to kill Rick now.

"Can we leave New Orleans? I don't want to be here anymore."

"Jules, I can't leave. I have to watch over Adam once the bond is paid. I'd get arrested if I let him run free. I promise you, that lady is a scammer. Just forget about it."

"Are you sure? Then how did she know we were newly-weds?" asked Jules.

"Your rings," said Rick.

"I didn't wear them. I didn't wanna wear them down here at night," said Jules as she waved her left hand for Rick.

That made Rick pause.

"Well, she saw mine," he said just as he remembered he had taken his off when he washed his hands in the hotel room and left it on the vanity.

Now Jules was really scared.

"Look, they make money scamming people and filling them with fear or hope. She's good at what she does. Nothing more, nothing less," said Rick, not even believing his own words at this point.

After a little more convincing, she began to calm down.

"Just promise me you'll be careful while we're here," said Jules.

"I'm always careful. I promise."

They continued to walk toward the hotel and stopped at

a red light, waiting for the pedestrian signal to light up. When it did, Rick took a step, and Jules accidentally dropped her shopping bag. A car ran the red light and slammed on its brakes, hitting Rick, and he rolled onto the street. It didn't hit him too hard; and he mostly lost his footing as he tried to jump out of the way.

"Rick!" yelled Jules as she ran up to him.

The driver saw Rick on the ground and turned right, peeling out and disappearing down the street before Jules could get the license plate number as it fled the scene. The hit-and-run driver was long gone.

"I'm okay, Jules. It barely touched me. I'm gonna have a little bruise on my left leg but that's it."

A crowd had gathered as Rick stood up.

"I'm okay, everybody," said Rick.

Jules' eyes were filled with tears.

"She was right."

"Oh my God, Jules. I should've looked before I stepped out. I wasn't paying attention. That's all. I swear."

Jules was sniffling as she held Rick's arm, and they crossed the street. Deep down, it had shaken Rick and the woman's words now made him nervous. They finally made it back to the room and Jules massaged the area the car hit on Rick's left thigh. It was already starting to blacken, so she got some Arnica from her overnight bag and rubbed it on the bruised area. After they undressed and climbed into bed, Jules held Rick tightly all night.

The next morning, Rick ordered some chicken and waffles to the room. He was famished. He poured Jules a cup of coffee and one for himself as they waited for room service. Rick tipped the man at the door and pushed the cart over by the window. He poured the warm syrup on the waffles and took a bite.

"Oh my God, so good. Try the chicken, Jules."

Jules cut a small piece of chicken and dipped it in the syrup. Rick took large bite of chicken and talked with his mouth full.

"I think today we need to..."

Rick got quiet and had a funny look on his face.

"Need to do what?" asked Jules urging him to finish his sentence.

Rick reached for his throat and started pointing toward his mouth. He had a piece of chicken lodged in his throat and couldn't breathe.

"You can't breathe?" asked Jules desperately.

Rick shook his head, and Jules ran behind him, wrapped her arms around his chest, and heaved as hard as she could. Rick was turning blue. She tried again, but he was too heavy for her. He was losing consciousness. She locked the fingers of both her hands, reached back and hit him as hard as she could in the upper back. He flung forward and spat out the chicken. His eyes were watery as he coughed. He stood up, gasped for air, and then hugged Jules.

"Thank you, thank you. I was starting to freak out," said an out-of-breath Rick.

Jules was crying like a baby and Rick held her tightly.

"It's okay now. It's okay. It's all over, baby," said Rick.

He knew Jules was taking the woman's words too seriously. He also knew he needed to chew his food better. It wasn't the first time he tried to swallow a piece of chicken that was too large. He was still hungry but settled for coffee instead. He knew Jules, was freaked out and had lost her appetite.

"I need to find a real voodoo queen. You need a gris gris bag. I'm going down to the Ninth Ward. You are staying here. Period!" demanded Jules.

"Jules, it's dangerous down there. I don't want you going alone."

"Fine, I'll take Chief and this," said Jules as she pulled her Springfield Hellcat 9-millimeter out of her purse.

"I should go with you," said Rick.

"If you don't get back in that bed and watch Netflix, I'm gonna shoot you myself," said Jules.

Rick made a scared face and climbed into bed.

"Please be careful. Where are you going exactly?" asked Rick.

"I'm going to the Voodoo Spiritual Temple on Rampart Street. I couldn't sleep last night while you snored away after being hit by a car. Nice bruise by the way," said Jules rocking her head in a cocky style.

"I've been there. I met Priestess Miriam before. She's the real deal. Be careful and hurry back. If you're not back in an hour I'm coming after you. You can shoot me if you want to," said Rick.

"I'll be back. She's expecting me."

Jules grabbed Rick's keys off the desk, picked up Chief,

and headed out the door. Through the door, she yelled: "Lock the deadbolt and don't go anywhere!"

Rick locked the door and crawled back into bed. He was proud of Jules. She was a strong, confident woman, and when she was on mission, no one could stop her. He was looking forward to getting the gris gris bag. That tarot card woman got his goat, and he was starting to question his safety.

Jules entered the temple and was greeted by Priestess Miriam's assistant.

"Please have a seat. She will be with you shortly."

Jules sat down and put her purse on her lap. A few minutes later, Priestess Miriam entered the room and lit some black candles.

"Tell me about your man," she said.

"His name is Rick, and he's a good man. We had our tarot cards read. She told Rick he was in danger, and ever since then, he has had two close calls," said Jules.

"Give me your hands, child."

Jules reached out across the table, and the priestess took her hands.

"I feel a great love from you to your new husband."

"How did you know he is my new husband?" asked Jules.

"Anyone with the power can feel that."

The priestess started chanting in Patois and a mix of French Creole. She pulled a small leather pouch from a wooden box on her shelf, along with a large box full of odd pieces of wood, a feather, a large silver coin, dirt, and items Jules couldn't identify. She continued to chant over them as she placed bits and pieces into the leather bag. She picked up the pouch, pulled the strings together to tighten it, and placed it on her heart.

"Give this to your man and do not open it for any reason. Make him carry it everywhere he goes until the full moon has risen. He will be fine after that."

"How much do I owe you?" asked Jules.

"My services are free for you, dear. You may place a donation for the children of the temple on your way out, but it's not mandatory. I'm glad to help. Please tell Mr. Waters hello for me. I remember him from the time he came here before."

"How did you know his last name was Waters? I never said that."

"His presence is with you, now and forever. You two are one."

Jules thanked her as she tried to hold back her emotions, folding five one hundred dollar bills and placing them in the donation box. Chief was still chewing on the hard plastic dog toy that Jules had handed him in the travel cage in the Jeep. She had cracked the windows when she stepped inside the temple. As she drove back to the hotel, tears gushed from her eyes, allowing her emotions to flow. She breathed deeply, and a sense of peace fell over her. Once back in the room, she told Rick what had transpired.

"Jules, I had the weirdest dream that I was at the temple with you and Priestess Miriam. I was hovering over the table that had three black candles burning on it. I watched her place a bunch of items in a leather pouch just like that one in your hand. She put a silver half-dollar inside."

"No fucking way!" said Jules in disbelief.

"Yeah, in my dream, it was 1959 half-dollar."

Jules handed him the leather pouch without mentioning that a silver coin was inside.

"Do not open it under any condition until after the full moon has risen. Priestess Miriam says hello, by the way."

TEN

Gary paid Jack five hundred thousand dollars and put a lien against his Prevost at AAA Bail Bonds. It was a lot of money, but he knew Rick would keep an eye on Adam. Adam wasn't going anywhere anyway. The judge would keep his passport and make him wear an ankle monitor. If he did run, Gary would hunt him down like a dog and bring him back himself, or, even better, he'd put Jules on his tail. Bounty hunting was her specialty, and she was the one in Rick's camp who was certified as a bail enforcement agent, aka bounty hunter. Gary planned to meet Rick and Adam's lawyer at the courthouse at 1:00 p.m. to speak to the judge and take over guardianship of Adam.

"Let's sit here," said Rick as he allowed Jules to step in front of him in the second row at the courthouse.

Jules sat down and looked around the room at all the men in orange jumpsuits. She spotted Adam, and he nodded at her. He was handcuffed and in shackles, sitting at the end of the designated prisoner seating area. It broke her heart. He had just lost his soulmate and was now being falsely accused of his murder. Rick nervously fidgeted as his heel rocked up and down extremely fast. Jules placed her palm on his leg to calm him down and felt the gris gris pouch in his right pocket. It made her smile. She leaned into him and whispered,

"Is that a gris gris bag, or are you just happy to see me?"

Rick smiled and winked at her. Gary walked in with Todd, and they sat in the front row. Gary looked over at Rick and Jules and waved with his head. Several inmates took the counsel table with their court-appointed lawyers, learning their bail amounts or being released on bond once it was paid. When Adam was called to the bench, Todd took a seat and spoke to the judge, providing proof that Gary had paid his bond. The judge reviewed the paperwork and instructed the bailiff to return Adam to the holding cell. Rick and the gang walked out of the courtroom. They all met in the hallway and discussed the next steps. Adam would be released from the detention center in a few hours, so Rick and Jules headed out to grab lunch and then pick up Adam after his release.

Jules drove the Jeep so Rick could read the paperwork the judge had given Todd. He was fully responsible for Adam, and if he failed to appear for any hearings or a trial, Rick could be arrested. He didn't like that part one bit; there was nothing he could do about it.

"Let's go to the Blue Crab. It's over on the lake, and I'm craving gumbo. Sound good?" asked Rick.

"Sure," said Jules as she told Siri to open Google Maps and take her to the Blue Crab.

The parking lot was quite full for 3:00 p.m. Jules followed Rick, scanning the area for potential danger. Jules was gonna protect Rick whether he liked it or not. They only had to get through another night until the full moon, and the danger would pass the next day. Rick still thought it was all a coincidence, but he played along with Jules to make her feel better. When they got upstairs, they sat at a table close to the band adjacent to the bar.

Rick ordered a plate of boiled crawfish and a bowl of seafood gumbo. Jules got a crab cake sandwich and a side salad. The waiter brought out a wooden cutting board with a fresh, hot loaf of buttered French bread. Rick scarfed down most of the bread before the crawfish even arrived.

"Slow down and chew your food!" demanded Jules.

"Yes, ma'am," replied Rick with puppy dog eyes.

The band was rocking. The guitar player was on fire with his smoking solos. He leaped around the stage like a madman. As Jules watched the band, a customer at the bar finished his steak and pushed his plate to the end of the bar. As if it all happened in slow motion, a napkin slipped off his plate and fell to the floor. The guitar player jumped up, and when he came down, his foot landed on the napkin, causing his leg to slide forward and trip a waiter walking toward the bar, carrying a tray of dirty dishes. When he fell forward, he reached for the bar, and his tray slammed against the knife hanging off the plate of the man who had just finished his steak. The sharp steak knife flew off the table and flipped through the air toward Rick and Jules' table. With the speed of an eastern diamondback, she picked up the empty wooden cutting board where Rick had just taken the last piece of bread. The knife stuck into the cutting board, inches from Rick's throat, and made a thunking, metal-resonating sound as it vibrated back and forth, stuck in the wood. Rick just sat there with bread hanging out of his mouth and his eyes wide.

"What the fuck?" exclaimed Jules.

The manager came over to make sure they were alright and apologized for the accident.

"I'm so sorry. That's a freak accident. I've never seen anything like it. I saw the whole thing from the bar. Folks, your lunch is on me. I'm just glad you're not hurt. How did you pick up that cutting board so fast?" asked the manager.

"Reflexes, I guess," said Jules as she handed him the cutting board with the knife still stuck in it.

Everyone who saw it happen shook their heads in disbelief.

"You need a suit of armor," said Jules.

Rick pulled the bread from his mouth, still shocked by what had just happened. He was at a loss for words. They finished lunch, and Rick tipped the waiter generously, even though the meal was free. As they headed to the Jeep, Rick received a text that Adam was set to be released in half an hour, so they went to the detention center. They sat in the waiting area, and within fifteen minutes, a guard walked out and unlocked the handcuffs and shackles. Adam was taken into a small room and allowed to change into street clothes.

Once he signed for his personal items, he was released into Rick's custody.

"Phew!" said Adam. "Boy, I'm happy to see you two."

"Let's get out of this shithole," said Rick as he patted Adam on the shoulder.

Once back at the hotel, Rick explained the rules to Adam about his so-called house arrest.

"Technically, we're supposed to be in the same house or room, but since we have adjoining rooms, as long as I keep the door cracked open between the two rooms, we should be legal. Don't run off, or Jules will shoot you."

She opened her purse, revealing her semi-automatic handgun, and winked at Adam.

"I won't go anywhere unless I am with you. You have my word. You and Gary have done so much for me. I am eternally grateful."

"It's all good, Adam. We believe in you, and we're going to get you out of this mess. We have to go to the set in the morning, so set your alarm for 6:00 a.m.; you have to go with me."

"Thanks, Rick."

Rick stepped through the adjoining door and left it slightly ajar. Although he trusted Adam, he realized he didn't know him very well. So, he placed a silent door alarm on the outside of Adam's room. If Adam tried to leave, Rick's phone would vibrate. It was a precaution, just to be safe. Rick and Jules went to bed early because they had to be on set by 7:00 a.m. When Rick's alarm went off, he didn't feel like getting up. He groaned as he climbed out of bed. He peeked into

Adam's room and heard the shower running. He checked his silent door alarm and saw that it hadn't gone off once. Rick made a pot of coffee and filled up both his and Jules' Buc-ee's travel mugs.

"You ready?" hollered Rick through the door into Adam's room.

"Yep, be right there," he replied.

Adam stepped through the door and followed Rick and Jules to the elevator. Adam grabbed a to-go coffee in the lobby. When they arrived on the set, they all went straight to Craft Services for breakfast. Gary and Possum were already sitting at a table.

"Hey stranger," said Possum to Adam. "I bet you're glad to be out, huh?"

"Oh man, you have no idea. I just feel bad that Rick has to babysit me."

"You're in good hands. Hey Rick. I just found out this morning that tonight is a full moon. Do you and Jules mind filming the scenes this morning and hanging out in the motorhome, so we can shoot one more tonight? It's early. I want the moon on the horizon," asked Possum.

Rick looked over at Jules and she shrugged as if she didn't care either way.

"Sure, we can do that. What about Johnie and Clay? Aren't they staying in the motorhome?"

"They left this morning. Clay has to take the new jet to Atlanta for some mods and Johnie offered to keep him company. They'll be back tomorrow or the next day."

"Perfect," replied Rick.

"Oh, and Rick. Now that you're playing more than a zombie extra, I wrote a new action scene with the sheriff. It's a shooting scene where a zombie picks up a pistol and starts shooting all over the place indiscriminately because he is, well, a zombie, then the sheriff takes out his silver-plated 44 Magnum and blows away the zombie. It'll be fun."

"That sounds awesome. Just make sure the guns have blanks. We don't want to make a *Rust, Zombie-style* movie," said Rick.

"We have the best gun techs money can buy," said Possum.

After breakfast, Jules got into makeup for her scene while Rick and Adam hung out and watched. They shot the scene five times for safety.

"Making movies is kinda boring," said Rick.

"All the takes can be a bit tedious for sure, but I find them fascinating. I've been on many sets with Paul," said Adam.

"I bet. How are you doing with that?"

"I'm okay. Life goes on. I know Paul would want me to carry on, so I'm trudging through."

"That's good to hear," replied Rick.

John, the wardrobe supervisor, knocked on Rick's motorhome door.

"Are you ready to be fitted for your sheriff's uniform?"

"Sure."

Rick and Adam followed him to the dressing rooms.

"What do I do with this?" asked Rick as he pulled out his personal Smith & Wesson 40 caliber Shield pistol.

"You can place it in this drawer. No one will mess with it," said John.

He pulled open the drawer, and Rick placed his weapon inside, then closed it. John then measured Rick and selected trousers, a shirt, and the rest of the outfit, including a felt cowboy hat. The silver revolver was beautiful, and the entire outfit looked realistic. The pants were so snug that he put the gris gris pouch in his front left shirt pocket to please Jules. Thirty minutes later, he was called to the set. The moon was just about to rise, so they wanted to run through the scene to ensure it all looked good. Possum decided to run the film just in case they got an awesome take; then they'd go again as the moon appeared on the horizon.

"Quiet on the set," said the AD.

"Action," called Possum.

Jules stood by Possum, watching as a feeble zombie ambled into view and picked up the nine-millimeter pistol lying on the hood of a burned-out car. He fumbled with it, managed to rack a bullet into the chamber, and inadvertently fired it, narrowly missing his head. Rick stepped in front of the camera, capturing an over-the-shoulder shot while another cameraman got his face. Rick delivered his line over the noise of the mindless zombie firing the gun randomly.

"If you fire a gun like that, you're gonna lose your head," said Rick.

He raised the silver-plated .44 Magnum and aimed at the zombie's head as the zombie continued to fire. Suddenly, Rick fell backward and hit the ground.

"Cut!" yelled Possum. "Rick, what are you doing? The zombie is supposed to fall down. Why are you improvising?"

Rick didn't move. Jules ran over to Rick, and he began to

groan and reached for his chest. Jules could clearly see a bullet hole in his shirt.

"He's been shot! Get a doctor, now!" yelled Jules.

Rick sat upright and unsnapped his left shirt pocket. He pulled out the gris-gris bag, which also had a hole in it. He loosened the leather string that kept it secure and dumped the contents into his palm. On top lay a silver half-dollar with a bullet hole impression pressed into it. Rick picked up the half-dollar with his thumb and forefinger.

"1959," said Rick as Jules' mouth fell open.

Jules helped Rick to his feet, and he had a massive bruise already showing up on the left side of his chest, right where his heart was.

"Are you okay?" asked Possum.

"Yeah, I'm gonna be sore as hell."

He pulled out his shirt that was tucked into his pants, and a spent bullet fell out and hit the ground. He picked it up and it was still warm.

"What caliber is that?"

"Hard to tell. The blank guns have smaller barrels, and while they can fire a real bullet, it would cause the gun to explode. The gun the zombie was using was a nine-millimeter. That looks like a bigger caliber bullet to me. I say a .40 or .45 caliber. You can send it to Carson, and they can do a ballistics test. That gives me an idea. Hang on," said Possum.

Jules wouldn't let go of Rick as he rubbed his chest. Possum walked over to the zombie from the last scene and picked up all the shell casings from the ground, emptied what was left in the chamber and magazine, and counted them.

"All casings accounted for. All blanks. That bullet came from somewhere else," said Possom.

Gary had already called an ambulance for Rick. He didn't need one but still required to be checked out at the hospital, as the liability insurance the producer was forced to purchase for the film mandated an ambulance ride for any accidents on the set. Possum called the day's shooting over and sent everyone home. Rick asked Jules to retrieve his pistol from the drawer in the dressing room and follow the ambulance in the Jeep to the hospital in Slidell. Adam rode with Jules. It wasn't protocol, but he wasn't going anywhere, and if he tried, Jules would bust his ass.

"Is Rick going to be okay?" asked Adam.

"I think so. He'll be sore. It was a miracle how that fifty-cent piece in his pocket saved his life. No, not a miracle. Magical," replied Jules.

"Is the gun tech going to be held responsible for allowing a live round to be loaded in the blank gun?" asked Adam.

"No, that bullet came from somewhere else, off in the woods, I think. Someone was either hunting nearby or intentionally shot at Rick. It didn't come from that blank gun. That's impossible. The gun would've exploded with a live round. They have smaller chambers not meant for real bullets. Only gunpowder charges according to Possum."

"I didn't know that. What about that girl who was killed on the set of *Rust*?"

"They were using real pistols on that set with blank shells. Somehow, a live shell was loaded in the gun that was used in the scene where she got shot. A tragedy and huge mistake. Possum would never allow real guns to be used," said Jules.

They arrived at the hospital and were told that the doctor would be out shortly. So, they sat in the waiting room. Jules was a mess; she was pacing back and forth. Adam tried to get her to sit down, but she was too filled with nervous energy. After about thirty minutes, a doctor came out and asked for Jules. She ran up to him.

"How is he?"

"He's gonna be fine. He will be extremely sore and have a massive bruise. We did an X-ray, and no bones in his chest were broken. He told me what stopped the bullet. That's nothing short of a miracle. The location of the wound is directly in front of his heart. He has a few documents to sign and he will be released shortly," said the doctor.

Jules thanked him several times and finally began to relax. After a short while, Rick appeared, and they headed back to the Jeep. Jules insisted on driving, which didn't bother Rick one bit. He was already extremely sore and knew it would get worse in a few days.

"Check this out Jules," said Rick as he handed her his iPhone.

He had taken a close-up selfie where the bullet had hit his chest. The outline and half-dollar could faintly be seen in his skin. When he zoomed in, the words LIBERTY in a circle on the top and IN GOD WE TRUST could be seen on the bottom, as well as a profile of Benjamin Franklin and 1959.

"Oh my God!" exclaimed Jules. "That's incredible."

"Take me to a tattoo parlor," said Rick.

"What? Are you crazy?" asked Jules.

"Some people say that. But I want that impression tattooed on my chest before it fades."

"Won't that hurt?"

"Nah, I'm pretty numb actually. The doc gave me some Percocet. I'm kinda flying right now."

Jules reluctantly looked up nearby tattoo parlors, and the one with the highest reviews was called Real Ink Tattoos & Piercings, which was not far from the hospital. They walked in and met the owner. Several people were getting inked when they arrived, but the owner, James, was free, and when Rick told him what happened, he personally agreed to do the work.

Rick sat in the chair as several customers and tattoo artists approached to see where he had been hit. He took out the coin and showed it to them. James went to work on Rick, tracing the impression made by the coin. He also looked at the real coin a few times for reference. It took less than an hour, but it was complete. James covered it with a specially moistened bandage and told him to leave it alone for a week. They left and headed to the hotel. After they arrived Rick got a text from Possum.

Check your email. I sent you a video. It was too large to text.

Rick opened his MacBook and saw the email from Possum. He clicked on the attachment as Jules stood over his shoulder. There was a small flash behind the zombie in the swampy woods to the left of the screen. Rick zoomed in on it and slowed it down seventy-five percent as directed by Possum. It was clearly the flash from the muzzle of a gun. It was no accidental shooting. It was attempted murder. He immediately called Carson in D.C.

"Hey buddy. It's Rick."

"Hi Rick. What's happening?"

"Can you do me a favor? I need a ballistics test done. Can I FedEx you a spent bullet from New Orleans?"

"I can do better than that. I have a friend in New Orleans named Woody Overton who had a podcast called "Real Life, Real Crime". He's a former detective for the Louisiana State Police. I bet he can pull some strings and get it tested locally. I'll give him a call and have him call you."

"Are you serious. I love that podcast. I'm a big fan. I think Johnie touched base with him on one of our cases before to get his opinion on something," said Rick.

"That's right. I forgot I connected those two. Woody will help you. I guarantee it. I'll call him now."

A half an hour went by and Carson texted Rick.

Standby, Woody will be calling.

Within minutes, Rick received a call from a 225 area code.

"Hello?"

"Is this Rick Waters?"

"Yes, it is. Is this Mr. Overton?" asked Rick.

"Call me Woody. Listen, I just got off the phone with our mutual friend Carson and he said you need some ballistics tests done."

"That's right," said Rick.

"Okay, I'm gonna call the firearms unit at the crime lab. I'm pretty sure you can run it by there tomorrow. Can I text you the go-ahead and address once I make confirmation?"

"Absolutely. Use this number you called me on. I'll also text you my email address. Oh, and Woody. I love your podcast. I listen often."

"Thanks, Rick. I appreciate you saying that. I'll be in touch."

They said goodbye, and Rick was beaming.

"I can't believe I just talked to Woody Overton. He sounded exactly the same on the phone as he does on the podcast."

Rick got the text from Woody within forty-five minutes.

He plugged the address into his iPhone and plugged it in to charge. Then he placed the half-dollar on his nightstand, while Jules ordered some food from room service. It had been a long day, and they wanted to chill out. Rick played with Chief until room service arrived. After dinner, they climbed into bed and called it an early night.

The next morning, Rick woke up before Jules, made a pot of coffee, and brushed his teeth. He wanted to get to the crime lab as soon as they opened. Jules yawned, looking extremely tired still.

"Baby, you don't have to go if you want to sleep in a little," said Rick.

"You don't mind?"

"Nah, I'll rake Adam with me. I'll be back before lunch I'm sure."

"Okay, be careful."

Rick filled his Buc-ee's mug with coffee and told Adam to get dressed. They left a few minutes later. Jules jumped out of bed. She was pretending to be tired. She wanted to get Rick a gift while he was gone to the crime lab. Before she went to sleep, she searched for custom jewelers nearby and found one called Sterling Silvia next to the French Market. She ordered an Uber, grabbed the half-dollar, and went down to the lobby. When she arrived at the jewelry store, she asked for the owner.

"Hi, my name is Jules and I have a special request. I need a rush order. Can you encase this coin in a sterling silver coin bezel and help me pick out a matching chain? I need it quickly. Like, within an hour. I'll pay extra for the rush."

"Darling, that's no problem. We have them in stock. I can have that done for you in about thirty minutes. It's straightforward and easy. Here are a couple of bezels to choose from," said the woman as she pulled out a display case and opened it for Jules.

"I like that one. It's for my husband and it's kinda rugged looking and will remind him of New Orleans," said Jules.

It was scalloped around the edges and had a fleur-de-lis bail at the top where the chain went through.

"I would suggest this anchor chain. Men love these and it would go well with the bezel."

Jules took one look at it and agreed.

"Do you want it to hang low or high?" asked the jeweler.

"Close to his heart."

"Is he average weight?"

"Yeah, he's in great shape, but he doesn't have a wrestler's neck or anything."

"Okay, let's go with a twenty-six-inch chain, and that way the pendant will hang right where his heart is. If you need to change it for a different length, just stop by within thirty days. It's no problem. If you wanna go grab a coffee or something, I'll have it ready for you within half an hour. I'll just need the coin."

Jules pulled the coin out of her pocket and handed it to her.

"Oh, my Lord, child. What happened?"

She told the woman the entire story and she was flabbergasted.

"Don't you worry. I'll take extra special care with this one. I'd normally polish the coin first, but I suggest we leave it natural under the circumstances."

"I agree," said Jules.

Jules walked across the street, grabbed a cup of coffee at The Market Café, and then strolled inside the French Market, perusing all the open-air shops. She found a couple of t-shirts she liked for herself and Rick and bought him a small voodoo doll as a joke. After a little more than half an hour, she returned to the jewelry store. The coin pendant was ready. It came out beautifully. She had the woman put it in a nice box with dark blue velvet. Jules was ecstatic about the way it came out. She paid the woman and ordered another Uber back to the hotel.

She placed the little jewelry box behind the tissue box on Rick's nightstand and eagerly awaited his return. While she waited, she ate some yogurt from the mini-fridge in the room and fed Chief some red grapes. A little while later, she heard Rick put his key card in the electronic door lock, and she bolted back to bed, pulled the covers over herself, and closed her eyes.

"I'm back," said Rick.

Jules yawned and stretched, feigning that she had just woken up.

"Wow, you're still in bed. I guess you needed it."

"I guess so," replied Jules, still sounding sleepy.

"I dropped off the spent bullet at the lab, and I should know something later today."

"That's great, Rick," said Jules as he sat on the edge of the bed.

"Did you move my coin?"

"No, I think it's behind the tissue paper," said Jules, biting her lip.

Rick picked up the tissues and saw the little jewelry box.

"What's this?"

"Open it and find out," replied Jules.

Rick slowly pulled the top of the little box off, revealing the pendant Jules had made for him. He gasped.

"You sneaky little angel. I love it! But how...?"

Jules pulled back the comforter, revealing that she was fully dressed.

"I took an Uber over to this place by the French Quarter and they made it for me. Put it on. I wanna see it on you. Take off your shirt first."

Rick unbuttoned his camp shirt and let out a soft moan from the soreness. Jules helped him fasten the clasp on the chain, and he stood up and turned around. It dangled perfectly where his heart was, just beside the tattoo.

"I can't believe you, Jules. That was so thoughtful. What gave you the idea?"

"I guess from that time we went to the Mel Fisher Museum in Key West, and you were admiring those Atocha gold coins on chains. I remember you saying that you'd rather find your own because it would have more meaning. The coin you are wearing saved your life. I'd say that has some meaning," said Jules.

Rick leaned over and kissed Jules on the forehead and hugged her tightly.

"Thank you, baby. I'll never take it off."

CHAPTER
ELEVEN

Rick checked his email, and the results from LabCorp had arrived. He downloaded the PDF and read through it. As he scanned down, he saw what he was looking for: a large amount of Gamma-Hydroxybutyric Acid was in Adam's system.

"I knew it! GHB. He was drugged. That's why he can't remember anything and woke up on a lounge chair by the pool," said Rick to Jules.

Rick immediately called Todd, Adam's lawyer, and gave him the news.

"Can you forward that to me? I need to give it to the prosecutor's office. It's a discovery, and I will push for a dismissal. They won't go for it, but I'm gonna do it anyway. Excellent work, Rick!" said Todd.

Rick knocked on the adjoining door to Adam's room.

"Hey Adam. I have a quick question for you. Have you ever taken GHB?"

"Is that a muscle supplement? I've taken HGH once when I got injured lifting, but I've never heard of GHB," replied Adam.

"GHB stands for Gamma-Hydroxybutyric Acid, and it is one of the most effective date rape drugs, leading to significant short-term memory loss. It's unfortunate that we can't find your Under Armor cup. I bet there are traces of GHB in it," said Rick.

"Yeah, someone took it. Damn!"

"We should have some more information from the ME office today on Jason Bagley. I'm gonna head down there later. However, I first need to obtain a power of attorney from Mrs. Bagley so I can speak with the ME and obtain the results. They have his body now at the Jefferson Parish Coroner's Office in Gretna."

"Wherever you go, I go," said Adam.

Jules decided to stay at the hotel and visit the spa. All that medical stuff bored her, and she was no longer fearful for Rick's safety now that the full moon had arrived the day before. Rick printed out a power of attorney at the hotel business office and went online to find a notary public in Gretna who made house calls. He called them up, agreed on a price, and provided Mrs. Bagley's address. Once he secured the signed power of attorney, they headed to the coroner's office. They arrived shortly after 1:00 p.m. After showing the receptionist the paperwork, she led them back to the ME's office.

"Hi, I'm Rick Waters, I'm a private investigator. I have a power of attorney for Mrs. Bagley, the deceased's mother.

Can you give me a copy of the new toxicology and autopsy report?"

"Sure. Let me print one up for you. I can also email you a digital copy." Said the medical examiner.

The man fired up his computer, and Rick could hear the printer making noise in another room. Rick gave him his email address, and the man forwarded the results to him. He retrieved the hard copies from the back office and handed them to Rick.

"It's quite an interesting finding. I changed the cause of death from accidental to murder, and the manner of death is incredibly intriguing. Take a look." The ME took his pen and pointed at one line.

Thallium.

"Thallium?" asked Rick.

"Yep, it's odorless and tasteless and rarely tested for. It's incredibly unusual to be found in the bloodstream and highly toxic. Since it was an exhumation, I did an extensive drug test panel. I had a hunch after I found the thallium and opened up the arm where the needle with the heroin was found. Come take a look."

Rick followed the ME to where the bodies were kept in the back. He pulled out the long silver drawer with Jason's body in it, then unzipped it and pulled back the white sheet, exposing his arm.

"Two things are odd here. That's why I changed it to murder. What strikes you as odd?" asked the ME.

"The discoloration of his muscles where you opened him up on his arm?"

"Exactly, he didn't OD. The needle didn't even hit a vein.

That discoloration is because he was injected post-mortem. And the other thing that you probably wouldn't have known is that he was left-handed, and the needle was injected into his left arm. Being left-handed, you'd think he would have used his left hand to inject his right arm. He'd have more control," said the ME.

"Plus, he hated needles, according to everyone who knew him," replied Rick.

"Bingo. Someone else injected him to make it look like an overdose. I included all those findings in my autopsy report and took lots of photos. If you need me to testify in trial, don't hesitate to ask."

"Thank you very much, Mr...?"

"It's Alberetti. Dr. Alberetti."

"Thanks, Dr. Alberetti. I'll be in touch if we need you," said Rick as he showed himself and Adam out.

"That's solid evidence. I think Jason was the killer; the murder part doesn't quite fit, but I bet his teeth cast matches the bite on Paul's face. We need to get that tooth cast from the New Orleans ME's office and test it against Jason's bite mark. I ordered a cast of Jason's mouth. It'll be back tomorrow. Maybe he felt guilty about killing Paul and took the thallium. To cover that up, maybe he shot up the heroin. But that doesn't make sense either because the ME said the heroin was injected post-mortem. Maybe he just missed and was on the edge of death. I don't know. I'm onto something big and I'm gonna figure it out. This will give the jury reasonable doubt, if nothing else. We don't have to prove you didn't do it; we have to plant enough reasonable doubt in the jury's mind that they won't convict you."

"I feel better about the case now, Rick. What's next?"

"We need to head to Mrs. Bagley's place and let her know her son didn't overdose."

They drove over to her house, and Rick explained everything to her. She acted relieved.

"Thank you, Mr. Waters. I appreciate what you did. Now I can put this all behind me once and for all and start the healing."

"I'm glad I could give you some closure, Mrs. Bagley," said Rick.

Rick and Adam walked back to the Jeep and then headed to the hotel. The moon wasn't completely full tonight, but Possum wanted to reshoot the sheriff scene. He could make the moon appear full in post-production. Rick texted Jules to meet them under the awning in front of the lobby. They picked her up and went to the refuge. The place buzzed with excitement as Possum filmed some graphic, flesh-devouring scenes with the paid zombies. He parked, and they all went into his motorhome. The wardrobe supervisor had already replaced Rick's sheriff's uniform with a new one. Rick locked his 40-caliber pistol in the motorhome's safe and changed into the uniform.

Possum sent a PA to bring Rick to the mark, and they filmed a take. It went perfectly, and the zombie's forehead exploded from a squib hidden under some latex skin that Richard had filled with a mixture of corn syrup, red food dye, and corn flour, known in Hollywood as 'Kensington Gore' because it was originally created by a British pharmacist in London specifically for special effects.

They filmed the same scene several more times with the

zombie wearing a green screen mask, allowing Possum to digitally remove his head in post-production. The special effects they could create were mind-blowing. After the shoot, Rick had an idea and called Adam's lawyer.

"Hey Todd. Do you know a digital forensics specialist who specializes in digital photography or image analysis? I would like to see if they can superimpose the photos from Paul's bite mark with the photos of Jason Bagley's teeth. Maybe even use the cast to check if they align. It's a shame they didn't swab the bite mark for DNA before Paul was cremated," said Rick.

"Yeah, but they did get a hit on an unknown male from the duffel bag and the murder weapon. On a hunch, I tested it against the known DNA of Jason, and it was an exact match. Unfortunately, those items also contain Paul's and Adam's DNA. So, it's not exactly a smoking gun, but it does show that Jason was involved. I think we have a strong case that shows Jason killed Paul because he was such an animal rights activist psycho and framed Adam. That's a motive. I wish we could prove that Jason was the one who put GHB in Adam's Under Armor cup. Without that cup, it's just an unprovable theory. The prosecution will try to contend that Adam did it to himself to create an alibi. I'll find a photographic forensic scientist and I'll get back to you," said Todd.

"Thanks, Todd. I'll be on standby."

"I'm hungry, Rick," complained Jules.

"Me too, baby. You mind if we do room service tonight? I'm still a little sore and wanna relax tonight," replied Rick.

"That'd be great."

Rick parked the Jeep in the garage, and they headed up to their room.

"Do you want to eat with us or in your room, Adam?"

"Today is Paul and my anniversary. I'm feeling kinda down. I think I need to be alone for a while."

"I'm sorry. Understandable. Knock if you need anything or want to talk. As I said before, order whatever you want from room service."

Rick and Jules had dinner while Chief sat in a chair next to Jules. She fed him small morsels of her meal, and he liked everything she offered him. He was a funny bird. Rick's phone buzzed; it was a new email. He opened it, and it had been forwarded from Woody Overton. It contained a PDF from the firearms unit at the crime lab. They determined that the bullet that struck Rick's coin was a 40 caliber.

That's weird. That's the same caliber as my gun.

Rick pulled his pistol from the nightstand drawer, where he kept it every night, and removed it from the holster. He sniffed it; it smelled like gunpowder. With all the excitement from when he had shot, that never occurred to him. As usual, there was a bullet in the chamber, so Rick ejected it, caught it in midair, pulled out the magazine, and counted the bullets. His gun had a seven-round magazine, but he only counted six bullets in total. There were only five in the magazine. One bullet was missing.

Could I have been shot with my own gun? I have to be wrong. It's impossible.

His gun had been in the dressing room during the filming when he was shot. Only two people knew it was in the drawer at that time: Adam and John, the wardrobe supervisor. Adam was on set, standing behind Jules, as far as Rick could recall. After Rick was in the ambulance, Jules retrieved the pistol, which remained in the drawer. Rick had no choice but to list John, the wardrobe supervisor, as a potential suspect. He didn't seem like that kind of guy, but then again, Ted Bundy didn't look like a sadistic serial killer, yet he was. The fact that a bullet was missing and that the gun still had a faint smell of gunpowder couldn't be denied. Rick always cleaned his gun after firing it. The last time he had fired it was at the range, and he remembered breaking it down completely, cleaning it thoroughly, and oiling it after returning from the range. What Rick needed was the spent shell casing. If he could find that, he could prove or disprove whether it came from his gun. He would head back to the set at sunrise, grab his Garrett metal detector from storage under the motorhome, and search for it in the woods. The Remington ammo Rick used was fairly common, so if he did find a Remington spent casing, it would still have to be tested against his gun. It was a small possibility that he had only loaded six bullets instead of seven the last time he reloaded the pistol.

After dinner, Rick and Jules went to the gym. Adam stayed in his room, but Rick would know if he left because of the silent alarm he had rigged on the door. He checked the app, and it was still active with ninety-eight percent battery life remaining. Jules worked out, while Rick just walked on the treadmill and sat in the sauna to ease the soreness from the gunshot bruise.

They returned to the room and went to bed early. Rick woke up, made coffee, and headed to the set in the refuge.

Jules would keep an eye on Adam. At this point, they had no reason to believe he would run. When Rick arrived, the only ones on the set were the security guards. Possum was asleep in the editing trailer. Rick unlocked the door to the basement storage of his motorhome, pulled out his metal detector and pinpointer, inserted fresh batteries, and watched the video Possum had sent him of the flash of a muzzle in the woods. He lined up the video with a specific tree and stepped into the woods. He began a round square search pattern. He found several fishhooks and some old-time beer can tabs. He stood by the tree and made a gesture with his hand, pointing to where he had been standing when he was shot, and tried to visualize the path of the spent shell. After adjusting his search area a little to his right, he began another sweep. On the third sweep, his detector went off. He swept over that area a few more times to dial in the spot better, then moved the grass aside. Something shiny glimmered, and he reached down and picked it up. It was a 40-caliber Remington casing standing upright in the grass.

"Son of a bitch!" he said aloud. "Gotcha!"

He let Possum sleep and headed back toward New Orleans before 7:00 a.m. He drove straight to the firearms unit of the crime lab, turned in his gun, the ammo, and the spent casing for testing. The forensics tech wrote down Rick's phone number and told him he would text him once he had the results. He figured he could get to it before lunchtime. Rick returned to the hotel, and Jules was in the shower. Rick could hear the TV on in Adam's room, so he peeked in and saw him sitting on the couch watching local news.

Rick made a fresh pot of coffee, called room service, and ordered two full breakfasts and one for Adam, too. After feeding Chief, he kissed Jules and told her that he found it, then jumped in the shower. When he stepped out of the shower, he noticed he missed a text. It was from Todd.

We are going to trial on Thursday. I already called Adam. Give me a call.

Rick quickly dried off and called Todd.

"Hey Todd. I saw your message."

"Can you and Adam come to my office? We need to prep for this trial. I've set up a war room and hired another lawyer to assist me. He specializes in forensics."

"Sure. What time?" asked Rick.

"Now, if you can. Or as soon as possible."

"Okay, I just stepped out of the shower. Let me get dressed, eat breakfast, and then we'll head straight over."

"Perfect. See ya soon," said Todd.

Rick got dressed and breakfast arrived a few minutes later. He knocked on the door to Adam's room.

"Hey Adam, I ordered us all breakfast. You wanna come over?"

"Sure. I'll be right there."

Jules set out all the meals on the dining table and poured some fresh coffee into three cups.

"Good morning, Adam," said Jules.

"Good morning, you two. Thanks for ordering breakfast, Rick."

"No worries. Listen, after we eat, we need to head over to Todd's office. I know he called you."

"Yeah, he told me."

"Are you okay?" asked Rick.

"I'm not going to lie. I'm feeling some anxiety."

"We have a great defense started," said Rick.

"Let me get something for you to help with anxiety," added Jules.

Jules dug through her overnight bag and found the old prescription bottle of Xanax she had gotten after she was carjacked in Mississippi. She didn't take them anymore but always felt better just having them with her. She grabbed Adam a bottle of water and handed him the little blue pill.

"What is it?"

"Xanax. It will take the edge off," replied Jules.

Adam took the pill, and they all ate breakfast. He was amazed that Chief liked scrambled eggs and sausage.

"He will freaking eat damn near anything. Avocados are poisonous to cockatoos, but other than that, he can have most anything," said Rick.

"Really? Avocados, huh?"

"Yep. There's something in the seed that can kill them."

"Interesting," said Adam.

After breakfast, Rick and Adam headed to Todd's office. Jules stayed behind, and Gary was going to give her a ride to the set. She had a full day of filming.

"Rick and Adam, this is Anthony Fieri. He is our forensics specialist. Let's all sit down and get to work," said Todd.

He had put up a large whiteboard so they could visualize everything they discussed. In large capital letters, he wrote two words and drew a line down the middle to create two columns. In one column, he wrote EVIDENCE and on the other side, he wrote DOUBT.

"Okay, so here's what we have on the left side so far: Adam's DNA on the murder weapon and duffle bag, means, opportunity, no alibi, cut on Adam's hand that matches the ligature. What am I missing?" asked Todd.

"Motive?" asked Rick.

"Exactly. That goes in the other column. I should also add in parentheses under DOUBT, (Alternate Suspect), aka Jason Bagley," added Todd.

"Smile at me, Adam," said Anthony.

Adam looked confused but flashed his white teeth at Anthony. Anthony took the eraser pen from Todd and, under DOUBT, wrote "TOOTH GAP" in "BITE MARK" before handing the pen back to Todd.

"The bite mark on the victim's face clearly shows a large gap between the cuspid and central incisor, also known as the eye tooth. The lateral incisor is missing. It's obvious that Adam is not missing any teeth and has a perfectly full smile.

"PHONE: Records show that Jason's phone was still on the set long after the filming for the day wrapped, and Adam's phone signal left the area just after filming ended. Your phone then pinged off a cell tower near the hotel where you and the rest of the crew stayed.

"MOTIVE: There is no motive for Adam to kill Paul. They were in a loving relationship, and Paul had no life insurance. Financial records indicate that you earned more money than Paul and had a substantial amount in a savings account in Copenhagen. Where did all that money come from, Adam?"

"My mother and father died in an automobile accident several years ago, and I am an only child. They left me everything," replied Adam.

"Would it be safe to say that you were well off before you even met Paul?" asked Todd.

"I felt comfortable. I have always been frugal and have rarely touched my savings, allowing it to grow over the years. So, yes."

"So, there is no motive for Adam, but there is a motive for Jason. He was an animal rights activist and had been arrested before for violent protests. The use of animal guts on the set as props for the zombie eating scenes made him angry. Angry enough to kill. That is motive!"

DNA: That has to go in both columns. But it clearly shows that Jason's DNA was on the murder weapon and the duffel bag, just like yours. I think we can convince the jury that you were drugged with GHB, and then Jason added your DNA afterward and disposed of the murder weapon and duffel bag in your hotel's dumpster. We can't prove that, but we can certainly provide reasonable doubt. The biggest hurdle we have to overcome is Jason's murder. Maybe there was an accomplice to Jason who got nervous and killed him because he thought they might talk if arrested. That is a complete unknown we can explore," said Todd.

"I can go over the list of extras and see if anyone else who was on the set the day Paul was murdered never returned. I believe there were three names, but I focused on Jason because he had a criminal record," said Rick.

"Great, Rick. We should have the results from the forensics image analyst of the photo overlays of the bite mark and Jason's dental photos."

"Awesome. Is there anything else you need us for today? I'd like to follow up on the list of extras," said Rick.

"No, Adam can stay here, and I will assume responsibility for him. I have some more things to go over with him, and I can drive him back to the hotel when we are done. Sound good?" asked Todd.

"That's fine. If he runs, shoot him. Ha-ha," said Rick jokingly as he patted Adam on the shoulder.

Rick drove back to the hotel to review the extras list. Jules was still on set filming. Rick scanned the list and found the other two names of people who had stopped coming to the set the day after Paul's murder. One was a woman named Janine O'Hara. After Rick did some research and found her online, he realized she had to be eliminated. She was five feet one inch tall and weighed one hundred six pounds. It would have been physically impossible for her to overcome Paul, who weighed over two hundred pounds, let alone lift his dead body into the freezer. The only name left on the list was Bill Hicklin. Bill was indeed big and strong enough to kill Paul so Rick went on NEXIS and researched him. He was a ghost. Rick couldn't find any info on a Bill Hicklin that matched his description and photo online.

Maybe he used a fake ID? But why?

Every extra had to have their photos taken before and after special effects were added to their faces, and they were fitted with a wardrobe. Those files were back at the set. He wanted to check on Jules anyway, so he drove out to the refuge. He waited for them to finish shooting a scene before greeting Jules. They had to do several more takes, so Rick found one of the PAs and had him show Rick where the extra's photos were filed. It took him a while to dig through the files but he eventually found Bill Hicklin's file. Inside the folder was a copy of his driver's license and the before and after photos of Bill. Rick used his iPhone to scan the photo. He knew a way to find out Bill's true identity.

"Hey Carson. I need a favor."

"That's what you say every time you call me. Ha-ha, shoot."

"I'm gonna text you a photo. Can you run it through the database and find a match with your facial recognition software over at Quantico?"

"Sure, no problem. I was heading over there soon anyway. I'm freelancing on a case for the FBI. I may be retired, but I'm not dead, and I still have my full security clearance. Go ahead and send it."

"Thanks, Carson. I owe you one."

"No, you owe me many, but I ain't worried about it."

Rick texted Carson the photo and watched Jules shoot three more takes. Once they wrapped up, he wanted to head over to the address on Bill's driver's license to maybe talk to him, so he waited for Jules to finish her makeup. She grabbed Chief from the motorhome, and they took off. His address was in Kenner, a suburb of New Orleans near the airport. Rick found the road, and Jules helped him look for the address. When they found it, Rick realized Bill had to be involved or was hiding his true identity for some reason. The house listed on the driver's license had flooded during Katrina and was boarded up, completely dilapidated, and in need of demolition. No one had lived there since 1995. Stumped, they returned to the hotel. Adam was still at Todd's office when Rick and Jules arrived at the hotel. Jules changed clothes, and they walked over to the Creole House Restaurant & Oyster Bar for dinner. Rick texted Adam to see if he wanted anything, and he replied that Todd had already had some sandwiches delivered and that they might be working a while longer. Rick had been to the Creole House many times before and was quite familiar with the menu. Before the waiter even brought them menus, he ordered the Gulf Shrimp Ya-Ya as a starter. It was a rich sautéed shrimp in pesto with Texas toast. A must-have when visiting the Creole House, as well as the bread pudding at the end. Rick thought they had the best bread pudding on the planet, and he was quite the connoisseur. Rick's phone buzzed before the entrées were served. It was Carson.

No match. He doesn't exist.

"What the fuck?" said Rick aloud.

"What's wrong, Rick?"

"That guy who used that run-down house on his driver's license has no match in the federal facial recognition database."

"Why not?" asked Jules.

"I don't know. He's either never been arrested or never owned a real driver's license."

"Maybe he's not from the U.S," said Jules.

"You freaking genius. I love you! I'll be right back."

Rick stepped outside because the restaurant was so loud. He called Renato, his buddy who ran INTERPOL in Italy.

"Hey Renato, it's Rick."

"Caio, Rick. Che si dice? What's up?"

"Can I text you a photo to run through the INTERPOL facial recognition database? I'm chasing a ghost," said Rick.

"No problem, my friend. Text it to me."

Rick texted the photo.

"I can run it for you in the morning. I'll call you if I get a hit."

"Thank you, Renato. I appreciate it."

"What's this I hear, that you got married. I wasn't even invited to the wedding?!"

"We eloped. Don't worry. We are going to have a huge celebration once we wrap this movie. You will be there. I promise!"

"Okay, then you're off my shit list. Ha-ha. I gotta run. Chat soon, ciao."

"Bye, Renato."

Rick stepped back into the restaurant just as the entrees arrived. During dinner, he and Jules discussed both the upcoming trial and the movie. They walked back to the hotel, and Todd texted Rick that they were on the way. Jules went up to the room while Rick waited in the lobby for Todd to drop off Adam.

CHAPTER
TWELVE

Rick, Jules, and Adam drove to the set. A full day of filming was scheduled. The trial was to begin in one day, and Rick still wanted to introduce more reasonable doubt into the case. While Jules got into makeup, he and Adam waited in the motorhome. Johnie and Clay got delayed in Atlanta and still hadn't returned. Adam asked Rick if he could step outside and watch the filming. Rick didn't mind since the set was surrounded by security and Adam hadn't tried to run once.

"Yeah, go ahead. This is tedious work anyway. You'd be bored sitting here," said Rick.

Trials typically took months, if not years, to begin. However, due to the heinous nature of the murder, the media frenzy, and the prosecution's request for a speedy trial—along with the judge's notorious corruption—it was moved up the docket with lightning speed. This was highly unusual, and despite Todd's efforts to request several continuances, all were denied by the judge. He was known to be a show-boat and a media hound, allowing cameras in the courtroom and seeking to be the center of attention. The cards were already stacked against Adam before the trial was set to begin. He had already been convicted in the court of public opinion because of the way the media covered the case. They made him out to look like a monster. Several of the newspapers had headlines like, *Real Life Zombie on Set of New Orleans Zombie Flick* and *Crescent City Cannibal Indicted*. Rick had his hands full. Rick got a text from Renato.

I got a hit, check your email.

Rick opened his email with great anticipation. He downloaded the PDF Renato had sent him. Bill Hicklin's real name was Friedrich Wagner. He was a German national and had served a five-year stint in Brandenburg-Görden Prison for manslaughter. The German justice system didn't use juries like in the States, they used a system of lay judges, also known as laypersons, to decide cases. The cause of death of his partner was strangulation. The murder victim was his domestic partner, and Friedrich's attorney convinced the laypersons that the death was accidental during an erotic asphyxiation event.

This gets weirder every day.

Rick quickly forwarded the findings to Adam's lawyer. Now they had even more reasonable doubt. Rick needed to locate Friedrich, who had just shifted from being an extra to a person of interest. Finding him wouldn't be easy; Rick wasn't even sure if he was still in the country. Rick needed Possum's help. He would have to wait until filming wrapped for the day, but not only was Possum incredibly skilled, he was also a critical thinker who often thought outside the box. All Rick had to go on was his photo and the alias of Bill Hicklin. He discovered that Bill had checked out of the crew hotel the day Paul was murdered, which was also the last day he appeared on set. That was suspicious. Rick decided to begin calling all the hotels in the area to ask for Bill. He contacted every hotel within a ten-mile radius of the crew hotel. It was like trying to find a needle in a haystack. If he had one fake ID, he probably had more. It was going to be impossible. After two hours of calling hotels, he decided it was futile. Possum had just wrapped filming for the day.

"Hey buddy. I need your help," said Rick.

"Step into my office, Amigo," replied Possum

Rick explained the situation with Friedrich and showed him the photo.

"Checking hotels will be a waste of time. He could have multiple identities. First, let's check the flights to Germany and see if we can find him on any manifests with his Bill Hicklin alias," said Possum.

"How the hell can you do that?" asked Rick.

"I'm a hacker, remember?"

Possum booted up his computer and accessed the dark web, launching a program he had coded and inputting Bill Hicklin's name into the system.

"Now we just let it run. It'll take about fifteen minutes."

While they waited, Possum showed Rick the dailies they had just filmed. Jules looked like a movie star. It was incredible. Possum's phone pinged, indicating it got a hit.

Possum clicked on the link.

"Check it out, he flew into New Orleans from Düsseldorf

Airport a month before filming started. There's a copy of his German passport. It's fake. Let me print it. There is no record of him flying out of the US."

"That's interesting," said Rick.

"No, you know what's really interesting? Adam and Paul are listed on the same flight manifest."

"What?!"

"Yep. I think you need to confront Adam."

"I plan to."

"I just got another idea. Maybe you should call all the local hospitals and see if there is a Bill Hinklin registered."

"Great idea, Possum. Thanks for your help, buddy."

Rick returned to his motorhome and Jules and Adam were sitting on the couch talking.

"Hey, Adam. How long have you known Bill Hinklin? Or should I say Friedrick Wagner?" asked Rick.

"Who?"

Rick repeated the names.

"I've never heard of those names before in my life. I swear."

"That's funny, he was on the same flight, you and Paul flew on when you traveled to New Orleans."

"So, did half of the production company. Some others flew in the day before and after," said Adam.

"Don't move," demanded Rick as he stepped out of the motorhome and back into Possum's editing trailer.

"Can you pull up the entire flight manifest from the flight you found Bill on?"

"Sure, hang on."

A few minutes passed, and Possum's printer started spitting out paper. Rick picked them up and checked his master list of the crew. Sure enough, he recognized several names on both his list and the flight manifest.

"Son of a bitch. Adam is telling the truth. I owe him an apology."

Rick put his tail between his legs and walked back to the motorhome.

"Adam, I'm sorry I was so abrupt. You were telling the truth. Why was Bill/aka Friedrich on the flight, though? He wasn't part of the crew."

"I have no idea. Maybe he was one of Paul's friends in the movie business. He knew a lot of people."

Rick showed Adam a photo of Friedrich.

"I remember seeing him on the set, he was one of the zombies, but I never spoke to him. Like I said, Paul knew a lot of people," said Adam.

"Fair enough. I'm truly sorry I doubted you."

"It's okay, Rick. I get it."

"It's been a long day. Let's go back to the hotel. Steaks are on me. Let's just eat in the hotel and call it a day," said Rick.

Rick felt terrible that he had accused Adam of hiding something. He told Adam to order any steak on the menu. After dinner, they returned to their rooms. Jules settled in for a Netflix movie, but Rick took that time to call every hospital he could find. He was up way past 2:00 a.m. and had covered all the major hospitals in Slidell, Kenner, Gretna, and everywhere else in the greater New Orleans area and had struck out. He reluctantly gave up and crawled into bed, snuggling up to the warm Jules, who was purring away.

The next morning, he woke up early and felt terrible from a lack of sleep. He brewed a pot of coffee, turned on the local news, and set the TV to mute. A reporter appeared, discussing budget talks in New Orleans and how potential cuts could impact the police department, fire and rescue, the morgue, and other agencies. A light bulb went off. He woke up Jules, kissed her, and told her he was stepping out and would be gone for a while. He drove down to the morgue in New Orleans, spoke to the receptionist, and asked the ME if there were any John Does. He lied and said his brother was missing, showing the receptionist a photo of Bill. After looking at several corpses, he struck out and checked the next closest morgue on Google. He struck out again in Metairie and Kenner, so he drove to the only one left, which was the St. Tammany Parish Coroner's Office in Slidell. He showed the photo of Bill to the coroner, and his eyes lit up. Rick followed him back to where they kept the bodies. It was Bill. He had massive contusions and a tire mark across his chest.

"I'm truly sorry for your loss," said the coroner.

"Thank you. He was my brother. What was the cause of death?" asked Rick, trying to act like he was grieving.

"The official cause of death is listed as undetermined, but by the looks of his injuries and where he was found, it appears that he was hit by an automobile and run over. See those tire marks?"

"Where was he found?"

"In an overgrown ditch beside HWY 90 near the crossroads of Industrial Parkway, there was a Parish mowing crew out, and one of the workers found him early in the morning. We have determined the time of death to be the night before between 7:00 p.m. and midnight."

"Did you do a toxicology test?"

"No, but since you are the next of kin, if you'd like one done, I just need some ID."

"I left my stupid wallet at home. Let me run home and I'll come straight back. I'd also like you to test for poisons, specifically thallium," said Rick.

"Why thallium?"

Thinking on his feet, Rick said, "He worked at a cement factory nearby, and he was about to expose them to OSHA for violations. Maybe this wasn't an accident."

Rick texted Possum as he sat in the Jeep.

I need two IDs right away for the coroner's office. One for Bill Hicklin and one for me. Use the name Randy Hicklin and the same address as Bill's fake ID.

10-4.

Rick drove back to the set at the refuge and when he arrived Possum had already printed the fake IDs.

"Hey Rick. Stop at Walmart and buy one of those heated laminators. Use the thickest thermal pouches they sell. Trace out your driver's license and use scissors to cut them out. They should work just fine for the coroner."

"You are freaking amazing!"

Rick stopped at Walmart and purchased the laminator. He plugged it into the outlet built into the Jeep and followed Possum's instructions. He drove back to the morgue and handed both IDs to the coroner. The coroner quickly made copies of them and told Rick that he'd be in touch with the results. Rick called Todd to tell him what he found out.

"Hey, Todd, can you talk?"

"Yeah, any chance you can come to the office? I found something I'd like to share with you."

"Ditto. I'm on my way."

Rick parked, found a spot in Todd's office parking lot, and stepped into the office.

"Hi, Todd. Let's talk."

"I did some research, and I found out that Jason had traveled to Germany several times over the past few years. I don't know what it means, but it is an interesting development. It could have just been for vacation because he flew into Munich around the time of Oktoberfest," said Todd.

"His neighbor told me he went to that, but I assumed he meant here, not Germany. I have some more news that's gonna blow your mind. It might create more questions than answers."

Rick explained everything he had discovered about Bill Hicklin, aka Friedrich Wagner, and they both decided it was pertinent information to add to the evidence files.

"Since that freaking judge won't allow a continuance, we will have to introduce it as a new exhibit once the trial has started," said Todd.

"Tomorrow will be a big day. How long do you think the trial could last?" asked Rick.

"Weeks, if not months."

Rick left and returned to the hotel. He forgot that Jules had a scene to shoot and assumed Gary took her and Adam to the set. Since the set was beyond the hotel and near the location where Friedrich's body was found, Rick decided to take his metal detector, which was still in the back of the Jeep, and search the area. Rick found the crossroad and could see the area where the grass had been trampled by the police and the coroner's van that had parked. He took out his metal detector and started sweeping the side of the road.

"Freaking beer cans!" said Rick aloud as he continued to search.

He spent a good thirty minutes searching and was about to give up when his detector beeped. He pulled back the grass and found a completely smashed Samsung Galaxy pay-as-you-go Vodafone phone. Essentially, it was a European burner phone. It wouldn't turn on, and it had been rained on. The only way to get into it would be to FedEx it to Renato and have the techs in Germany crack it and recover the phone records. That would require a warrant and take considerable time. Rick texted Renato and asked him where to send it, then found the closest FedEx office and sped off toward it. He boxed it up and paid the woman behind the counter. He just hoped it would shed some light on the case and prayed that the info would arrive in time. Rick headed to the set to watch Jules work.

"Jules, I really want you to dig deep inside on this take. I want you to find hatred for all of mankind and use your power to raise the dead from their graves. The one person you raised from the dead has infected many others, but you want it to happen faster because you were persecuted by man, and now you want to destroy all living things," said Possum.

"I don't know if I can do that," said Jules.

"Why not?"

"It's way too evil," replied Jules.

"It's just a movie. You keep forgetting you're the bad guy in this one. I know that goes against your personal beliefs, but it's make-believe. If we ever do another movie, we'll make you the good guy. The hero. Deal?" asked Possum.

"Okay, I'll try. But if we do make another movie, I wanna be a badass hero. Like Lara Croft or Sarah Connor in The Terminator."

"Can do!" replied Possum.

Jules took a deep breath and tried to feel anger inside so she could summon some sort of evil to experience the revenge that this scene required from the character. She didn't have a mean bone in her body. So, she dug deep and remembered the time she was carjacked and how the guy belittled her and tried to make her feel like a useless human being.

"Okay, I'm ready," she said.

She went back to one, and Possum called action. Jules read the spell she had memorized from the script.

"Papa Gede, keeper of the gate,

Hear me now; I conjure fate.

With veve drawn and blood as a sign,

I call the dead, both yours and mine.

By bone and root, by ash and flame,

By shadow deep, I name their names.

Rise from sleep, O dust and clay;

The veil is thin; come forth and obey.

Spirits wandering, lost and bound,

Shake the earth and break the ground.

Flesh may fail, and time may lie,

But the Queen commands—you shall not die.

Come forth, the night is yours to dance;

By drum and fire, take your chance.

The living fear what death has known,

But through my will, you walk alone."

"Cut!" said Possum. "That was perfect, Jules. I really felt that take. That's a wrap for today, y'all."

Rick checked his watch, and it was almost 6:00 p.m. After Jules got out of makeup, he rounded her and Adam up and they headed back to the hotel. The trial was to begin in the morning. Rick dropped off Jules at the hotel, and he and Adam headed over to Todd's office to review everything and conduct a recap before the trial.

"Come on in, y'all have a seat in the conference room. We'll be right in," said Todd.

Rick and Adam sat down, and Rick took out a folder of everything he had done so they could compare notes. A few minutes later, Todd and Anthony joined them and closed the door to the conference room.

"Okay, let's begin. We're not going to be here late tonight because we all need a good night's sleep to be fresh. I have purchased a few suits for you, Adam. They are in the closet in my office. Take them with you when you leave. I used data from a focus group conducted in a study to choose the colors and styles that make a jury view a defendant more favorably, right down to the tie width and color. Wear the blue one in the front tomorrow," said Todd.

Adam nodded and thanked him. Rick knew Gary would be charged for the suits but it was important.

"So, we are going to focus on two things in this case. One, a potential other suspect, Jason Bagley, and two, a botched investigation by the Orleans Parish Sheriff's Department detectives. I plan to show the jury that they focused on you from the very beginning and never considered alternative suspects. They had blinders on for you and had tunnel vision from the very start of their investigation. Rick, we got the results back from the dental scan of Jason against the bite mark on Paul, and it is pretty much an exact match. The gap in Jason's teeth lines up with the bite. Adam, I want you to make sure the jury gets a chance to see your smile from time to time. Not any kind of creepy smile, but I'll ask you questions that would make anyone smile, so it seems normal. Just make sure you are looking in the direction of the jury. At some point, I will introduce the photos and bring in our image forensics specialist, as well as a forensics odontologist to verify the match. The state will try and make the jury think it is junk science so that's why I'll bring in each expert at separate times to drive it home. Rick, have you gotten the toxicology report back yet from St. Tammany Parish yet?"

"No, but I expect it to be emailed to me in the morning. I will forward to you the minute it arrives."

"Adam, there is no easy way to say this so I'm just going to say it. The court has deemed this a capital murder case with extenuating circumstances, and they are seeking the death penalty. It doesn't change anything. The stakes are just a little higher. Let's focus on getting you an acquittal," said Todd.

Anthony stood up and took over the conversation.

"Rick, doing that second tox test on Adam was pure genius. Finding GHB in his system will show that he was a victim and not the perpetrator. We're going to go hard on that. The house where Jason was found overdosed can now be searched by us. I got approval from his mother a few hours ago. Can you go search it for anything that can tie Jason to the murder, Rick? The police never searched it because they thought it was just another overdose, but since the coroner, as you know, found thallium in his system, his death has been ruled a murder and they are going to open an investigation. We need to get the jump on searching the house before the Orleans Parish detectives contaminate the crime scene," said Anthony.

"I'll go there tonight as soon as I leave," said Rick.

"Okay. Here is the key and a signed, notarized permission letter Mrs. Bagley gave to me."

They reviewed every detail of the case, and Todd did his best to put Adam at ease. Rick grabbed the suits from the closet, and they left, bound for Gretna. When they arrived, Rick made Adam wait in the Jeep. The last thing they wanted was for Adam to touch anything in the house and leave DNA behind. Rick donned latex gloves and used the key to open the front door. He began the tedious job of searching for anything that might link Jason to the case. He checked all the drawers and went through Jason's pile of mail. Rick spent over an hour searching the house and was about to give up when he stepped on a board in the kitchen, and it creaked.

He stopped in his tracks, looked down, and rolled the rug back. One of the boards on the hardwood flooring was loose. He pulled the rug completely out of the way and used his knife to dig into the edge of the wood to pop it up. Underneath the floorboard was a shoebox shoved between the joists.

"What's this?" asked Rick.

He lifted the lid off the shoebox and there was something wrapped in a towel. Once he unwrapped the towel, he couldn't believe his eyes. It was Adam's Under Armor cup with his name engraved on it just as he had said. Rick could hardly contain himself. He took photos and videos of what he had found and called the sheriff's department. He wanted them to find it, so he put it back where he found it and waited for the detectives to arrive. He knew the best way to get them there was to let them know a private detective was already searching the house. They hated private detectives. He had every right to be there but he wanted a witness, so he dialed the non-emergency number and spoke to someone in charge. Now all he had to do was wait. He went back to the Jeep and parked down the street. Within an hour an unmarked car arrived. Rick pulled up behind it.

"I'm Rick Waters, private detective. I'm here on behalf of the family. Are you here to investigate the murder?"

"Yeah, I'm Patrol Sergeant Jacobs. I here to assist the detectives and secure the residence"

"Do you have a warrant?" asked Rick.

The sergeant stammered and stuttered.

"Uh, uh, the detective will have one when he gets here, I think."

"That's okay. I have this. You are welcome to join me," said Rick as he showed the sergeant the key and the permission letter.

He followed Rick to the front door. Rick took his time pretending to search through the same items he had already looked over as the sergeant followed him around. When Rick entered the kitchen, he searched all the cabinets and drawers, and when he turned around and walked toward the sergeant, he stepped on the wooden flooring, which creaked beneath him.

"What's that?"

The sergeant tilted his head sideways, much like a dog does when it's confused. Rick rolled back the rug and used his pocketknife once more to pry up the loose panel. The sergeant leaned in closer, and when Rick pulled out the shoebox, his eyes widened. Rick set the box on the kitchen table and opened the lid, revealing the towel. He slowly unwrapped it and used the acting skills he learned on set.

"What the fuck?! This is Adam's cup. How did it get here?" asked Rick.

The sergeant was blown away.

"Do you have an evidence bag?" asked Rick. "We need to test this at the lab. No? That's okay we can use one of mine."

The sergeant was beaming with pride as if he had found the cup himself. Rick put the cup inside a plastic bag and labeled it. Rick had been filming the entire search with his Meta RayBans.

"Do you want to take it to the lab, or should I do it?" asked Rick.

"We have to wait for the detective!" demanded the sergeant.

"Good idea," replied Rick.

Rick didn't trust the sergeant or the detective, so to ensure that he would follow through, he asked him,

"You have this on the record, right? With your body cam? Does it have a timestamp?"

"Of course. It's been on the entire time."

"Me too," said Rick as he tapped on the side of his Meta glasses.

The detective smirked and seemed perturbed that Rick had also been filming. A few minutes later, two detectives arrived. The sergeant explained to them what had transpired, and after another search, they took the evidence in the bag and returned to their unmarked car. Rick followed close behind.

"Are you taking that directly to the lab?" asked Rick.

"Yeah, we can log it in as evidence."

"Great, I'll just follow you so I can get the tag number for the court."

The detectives were not happy. They had apparent disdain for Rick. Once the lab tech logged in the cup, Rick sarcastically thanked the detectives for all their fine work. He told the tech to test the cup for GHB, then returned to the Jeep and called Todd.

"Todd, I found Adam's cup in Jason's house. It's all on the record. It will be tested for GHB. If it shows up positive, we have our smoking gun," said Rick.

"Rick, you are the man! Now go back to the hotel and get some rest. We need to be fresh in the morning."

CHAPTER
THIRTEEN

"All rise," said the bailiff.

The sound of feet scuffling could be heard as everyone stood up in the courtroom, along with a few coughs and murmurs. Every seat in the courtroom was occupied. The trial was so popular that a lottery system was used for public seating each day. Several cameras were set up on tripods to film the proceedings. It was a shit show, to say the least.

"The Superior Court of Louisiana, Orleans Parish is now in session, the Honorable Judge Matthew Morgan presiding," said the bailiff.

"Good morning. Please be seated," said the judge.

Everyone took their seats in anticipation. There was an electric energy in the courtroom.

"This is case number 2024-CR-1185, The People versus Adam Olsen. We are here for the commencement of trial proceedings. Let me remind all parties—this courtroom is a place of order, respect, and the rule of law. Any disruptions will be handled accordingly."

The judge adjusted his glasses and looked toward the prosecution.

"Counsel, is the state ready to proceed?

The prosecutor stood up.

"Yes, Your Honor. The People are ready."

Judge Morgan then turned toward the defense.

"Defense counsel?"

"Yes, Your Honor. The defense is ready," said Todd.

Judge Morgan gave Todd a nod, then leaned forward slightly.

"Very well. We will begin with jury selection. Bailiff, please bring in the potential jurors."

The bailiff stepped toward the side door as the potential jurors began to file into the courtroom.

"Madam Clerk, please call the roll of the potential jurors," said the judge.

The clerk began reading the names. One by one, jurors responded and took their assigned seats in the jury box. Once all were seated, Judge Morgan addressed them.

"Ladies and gentlemen of the jury, thank you for your attendance today. Choosing a fair and impartial jury is one of the most critical steps in ensuring justice. This phase is called voir dire, and during it, both the prosecution and the defense will have the opportunity to ask you questions. These questions are designed to help determine whether you can judge the facts of this case fairly and without bias."

The judge glanced toward the prosecution table.

"Counsel for the People, you may begin."

The prosecutor rose and began his round of questions—brief, calculated, and professional. He was a tall, thin white man in his mid-sixties with a receding hairline. He had a strong southern accent; not Cajun, but he sounded more like he was raised in southern Georgia. Todd had done his research on the prosecutor. He moved to New Orleans from Savannah fifteen years ago and had assumed the role of assistant DA for Orleans Parish seven years earlier. After several rounds of questions, he thanked the jury and returned to his table next to the jury box.

"Mr. Thomas, you may proceed," said the judge.

"Good morning, ladies and gentlemen. My name is Todd Thomas, and I represent the defendant, Mr. Adam Olsen. Now, before I begin, let me remind you of something important—my client is presumed innocent unless and until the prosecution proves otherwise. That's the foundation of our system: innocent until proven guilty, not the other way around."

Todd paced slowly in front of the jury box, making eye contact.

"I want to talk to you a bit about fairness. Not the kind of fairness we hear about in commercials or political speeches, but the kind of fairness that lives right here in a courtroom. The kind that demands you keep an open mind, listen to all the evidence, and wait until the end before reaching any conclusions. That kind of fairness. Now, I'd like to ask a few questions. And there are no wrong answers. I just ask that you be honest. That's all we can ask of you."

He turned to Juror #4, a black woman in her fifties with sharp eyes and folded hands.

"Ma'am, have you or anyone close to you ever been accused of a crime?"

"Yes. My son-in-law was arrested a few years ago."

"I'm sorry to hear that. Do you feel that experience might make it difficult for you to remain impartial in this case?" asked Todd.

"I don't think so, but... I guess it depends on the evidence," she replied.

"Fair enough. That's all I can ask. Thank you ma'am."

He turned slightly, now facing Juror #7, a younger white man with crossed arms and a rigid posture.

"Sir, have you heard or read anything about this case before you entered the courtroom today?" asked Todd.

"I saw a headline when it happened. Didn't read much into it."

"Do you remember what the headline said?"

"If I recall, it said something like, Crescent City Cannibal Arrested," said the juror.

"The exact headline was, Crescent City Cannibal Indicted. Does the defendant look like a cannibal?"

"What does a cannibal look like?" asked the young man.

"Fair enough. And based on that headline alone, do you feel you've formed any opinion about Mr. Olsen's guilt or innocence?" asked Todd.

"I know there's more to it than a headline. You can hardly believe anything in the newspaper these days. It's all so sensationalized and biased."

"That's the right attitude. Thank you."

He's a keeper.

Todd's line of questioning, moving calmly and purposefully, probed for bias, clarified misconceptions, and gradually shaped the panel that could determine his client's future. Judge Morgan observed with quiet intensity from the bench, noting the jurors' reactions. The jury selection continued until recess, after which everyone broke for lunch. They would reconvene in a little over an hour and a half. Todd, Anthony, Adam, and Rick walked together to Coffee Science, a small café on Broad Street to eat lunch and discuss the jurors. That café would ultimately serve as their war room for the rest of the trial. Gary and Jules joined them after they all sat down.

"What you think so far?" asked Rick.

"I like Juror #4 and #7. Number 9 is history. She has already convicted Adam in her mind. Do you agree, Anthony?"

"Definitely. I wish we could've moved the trial, but that judge is an egomaniac, and he wants his face on TV."

"How are you holding up, Adam?" asked Todd.

"To be honest, I find it all incredibly interesting. It's so different from the way trials are held in Copenhagen. I've never attended one in person, but I've seen plenty in movies and TV shows."

"Well, good. We are in for a long trial and I want you to stay positive. That's half the battle," said Todd.

After lunch, Gary took Jules to the set, while Rick walked with Adam and the defense team back to the courthouse for another round of jury questioning. It was a long, drawn-out process, and by the end of the day, Todd had settled on just six jurors. It would be a battle royale between him and the prosecution to agree on the jury. Rick took Adam back to the hotel, and they waited for Jules to return with Gary from the set. While they waited, Rick asked Adam if he wanted to go to the gym. He did, and together they worked out. Rick learned some more kettlebell routines, and Adam burned off steam and let go of some of his anxiety. They each returned to their rooms, and Rick fed Chief and let him sit on the balcony to get some fresh air. Once Jules returned, Rick ordered room service, and Adam chose to eat in his own room. Rick couldn't imagine what was going through Adam's mind. The pressure must've been overwhelming. He respected his privacy and knew it was Adam's situation to deal with; all Rick could do was support him the best way he could.

Rick stood up from the hard wooden bench as the bailiff announced the arrival of the judge. The state and defense took turns questioning the jurors. Rick scanned them all, looking for anything he might notice that he could mention to Todd to aid in his choice.

Todd rose from his seat slowly, understanding the power of timing. His dark blue suit was tailored yet understated, and the knot of his tie was slightly loosened, suggesting he wasn't there to impress anyone but to do his job well. He stepped away from the defense table and approached the jury box, scanning the seated panel. His client, Adam Olsen, sat behind him, his expression unreadable and his hands folded on the table. Todd paused for a moment, hands clasped in front of him, allowing the jurors to settle into his presence. Then, his eyes landed on Juror #11. She was a woman in her early fifties, with soft features and some silver mixed in her dark hair. She wore wire-rimmed glasses, and Todd had already noted the way she had been watching everything—quietly and attentively, like someone accustomed to reading between the lines.

He smiled gently. "Juror #11—if I may—I'd like to ask you something. You mentioned earlier that you work in education. Is that right?"

She nodded. "Yes. I teach fifth grade."

"Fifth grade," he repeated. "That's a tough age. I imagine you deal with a lot of... let's say, conflicting stories?"

A small chuckle passed through the jury box, and the teacher smiled. "You could say that."

"So, when two students tell you very different versions of what happened on the playground, how do you sort through it? How do you decide who's telling the truth?"

She leaned back slightly, "I listen. I ask questions. Usually, one of them leaves something out, and sometimes both do. I try to stay patient. If I react too quickly, I miss the whole picture."

Todd nodded, pleased. "That sounds like the careful attention we need in this room. Thank you."

He turned, his shoes clicking softly on the polished wood floor, and stopped in front of Juror Number twelve. He was a younger man in a utility company uniform; arms crossed loosely over his chest. He hadn't said much during the earlier questioning, but Todd had noticed how he watched the attorneys, calculating, but not hostile.

Todd lowered his voice a little, quieter now and more

personal. "Sir, let me ask you something directly. And I'm not trying to put you on the spot, just asking for honesty." He gestured toward the defense table, toward Adam. "Do you believe someone is probably guilty just because they're sitting in that chair over there?"

The man tilted his head slightly, looking a bit uncomfortable, frustration crossing his face. Then he shook his head. "No. Not necessarily."

"Why not?" asked Todd.

"I mean..." The man raised one eyebrow. "I've seen how things go. People get accused all the time of things they didn't do. Maybe it's a mistake. Maybe someone lies. I don't think you can just look at someone in court and assume they're guilty."

Todd gave a slow nod, letting the juror talk. "And if you were selected to serve on this jury, would you truly be willing to hold the prosecution to their burden of proof? You would not convict unless they prove it beyond a reasonable doubt?"

The man's answer came without hesitation. "Absolutely. That's their job. Not mine."

Todd smiled. "Exactly right. Thank you."

He turned back toward the bench. "No further questions for these jurors now, Your Honor."

Judge Matthew Morgan, seated high behind the bench in his dark robe, gave an understanding nod. His expression revealed nothing, but his eyes missed nothing either. "Very well," he said, "Counsel, please approach for any challenges."

As Todd approached the bench, he let out a slow breath he hadn't realized he was holding. The jurors didn't know it yet, but the battle for Adam Olsen's future had already begun —in glances, tone, and questions that went deeper than they seemed. The jury selection lasted until 5:00 p.m. It could take days, even weeks, to select the right jury, but Todd was confident in the choices he had made. It all depended on the state's rebuttal.

"Your Honor, may I approach the bench before we recess for the day?" asked the prosecutor.

Both Todd and David approached the bench and whispered to the judge. They exchanged comments for a few minutes and then returned to their tables. Todd winked at Rick and had a small smile on his face.

"Ladies and gentlemen, both the defense and the state have agreed on jury selection as well as two alternates. We will recess for today and return in the morning to begin arguments. The jury is sequestered and reminded not to discuss the case outside of this courtroom with each other or anyone else for that matter. Do I make myself clear?" asked the judge.

The jury nodded as the judge struck his gavel on the wooden block, the sound echoing through the courtroom. Everyone exited, and a herd of reporters thrust microphones in Todd and Adam's faces, asking all the expected questions. Todd remained dignified, repeating several times that he and his client had no comment. Rick and Adam followed Todd and Anthony back to his office.

"Why were you smiling?" asked Rick after they sat down in the conference room.

"When I approached the bench, I got the vibe that the prosecutor thinks he has an open-and-shut casea slam dunk.

He's cocky and arrogant, but he has no idea what he's up against. It's not time to break open the Champagne yet, but he is underestimating my team, and we have something they don't have."

"What's that?" asked Adam.

"Rick Waters! That's what. I got the report back from the Under Armor cup. It tested positive for GHB. I will introduce it as evidence in the morning. It's gonna send the state into a tailspin. I'm giddy thinking about seeing his face when I introduce it as discovery."

"You're making me blush," said Rick. "I'm gonna call down to the St. Tammany Parish Coroner's Office and see if they have an update on the toxicology report for Friedrich. If we get it soon, maybe you can introduce that as well and give him a double whammy!"

"Wouldn't that be something? Anything to take that smug look off his face," said Todd.

Rick walked out of the conference room and called the coroner. He returned a few minutes later, shaking his head.

"Nothing yet. He said it could be anytime now, though, and he will email me. I'll forward it to you, Todd, as soon as I get it."

"Thanks, Rick."

They discussed the strategy for the next day's trial, and once they were finished, Rick and Adam returned to the hotel. Adam went to his room to read while Rick updated Jules on the jury selection and the current status of the proceedings. They decided to eat in the room, but instead of room service, Jules used Uber Eats to bring them shrimp PoBoys with French fries and red beans and rice from Liuzza's by the Track. Chief chowed down on fries, eager to eat every fry in Rick's Styrofoam container if he would let him. When the food arrived, Rick invited Adam to join them, and he did. Over dinner, Rick asked Adam about his experience growing up in Denmark. Copenhagen was a city Rick had never visited but always wanted to.

"I went to Rysensteen High School in Denmark. The city is very progressive or woke as some call it here in the US. I knew from an early age I was different. My parents were supportive of me when I came out. I first knew I liked boys when I was in wrestling. Luckily, I was accepted for who I was at an early age. I know it's much different here in the States, especially in the South, but it's coming around," said Adam.

"What kind of hobbies did you do besides sports growing up?" asked Jules.

"I was into photography for a while, but once I took chemistry in school, I was hooked. It wasn't really a hobby per se but more an infatuation with science. I graduated from high school as valedictorian and received an academic scholarship to the University of Copenhagen. I graduated with honors and earned my PhD in Organic Chemistry. That, along with my love for exercise, led me to personal training. I was working on my own line of health supplements, and Paul was going to help me get funding through some of his Hollywood contacts. I want to put out my own line of health products," said Adam.

"Dang, you're a smart feller. You know how to mix compounds and create your own muscle-building supplements?" asked Rick.

"Not just muscle building supplements but also recovery formulas for post workouts. I can make you some if you wish. That's what I always drink after a hard workout."

"You should talk to Gary about that. He's an angel investor and would probably love to help you get your product line off the ground once we put this trial behind us," said Rick.

"Really?" asked Adam as his eyes lit up.

"No shit. He's started several companies for and with other people."

"That would be amazing. Since I have my license, I can order compounds and chemicals that most people can't obtain unless they are a doctor or research chemist. So if you want me to make you something suited for your workouts, Rick, consider it done. I have access to almost any chemical because of my PhD. Plus, I know how to do it outside of a lab. I just need a few items like beakers and a Bunsen burner, etc. I can do it in my room."

"That's cool," said Jules.

After dinner, they called it a night, and Rick walked through the adjoining door.

"See you in the morning. Tomorrow should be an eye-opening day. Good night, Adam."

"Night, Rick. Thanks for everything."

CHAPTER

FOURTEEN

Rick received a notification about a new email, and when he opened it, he saw that it was from the coroner's office in Tammany Parish. He downloaded the PDF, and just as he expected, a lethal dose of thallium was found in Friedrich's blood. Rick forwarded it to Todd. Rick and Adam grabbed coffee to go, and Rick patted Adam on the back, telling him to hang tight, saying it was going to be a good day in court for him. Once the bailiff introduced the judge and the day's proceedings began, Todd stood from the defense table and addressed the bench. "Your Honor, the defense has two new pieces of discovery we believe are relevant to the case against my client."

Judge Morgan looked up. "Go ahead, Mr. Thomas."

Todd walked over to the evidence cart and held up a sealed plastic bag. "First, this is an Under Armor athletic cup recovered in the home of Jason Bagley, an extra on the set of the film my client's domestic partner worked on as an assistant director. Forensics found traces of GHB inside. We believe this was used to incapacitate Mr. Olsen at the hotel where some the extras and the entire crew stayed."

There was a small stir in the courtroom. Todd pressed on. "GHB leaves the system quickly. But when Mr. Olsen's blood was tested, trace amounts of GHB were found in his system. This cup—confirmed to be his—shows someone may have drugged him without his knowledge."

Prosecutor David Reed stood up, looking at Todd sidelong but saying nothing, arms crossed. Todd handed the item to the bailiff, who brought it to the judge—an accident report from the Louisiana Highway Patrol.

Judge Morgan looked at the report. "You're saying someone else on that set may be targeting cast members? I'll allow it as new evidence. Bailiff, please label this evidence as Exhibit 7A."

The bailiff followed the judge's orders, and Todd continued.

"Yes, Your Honor. I believe someone intentionally ran over Bill aka Friedrich Wagner with an automobile, and I am having his blood tested at the lab. He may have been poisoned first. If someone was targeting Todd with GHB, we believe it raises reasonable doubt that Adam Olsen killed Paul Strasberg. In fact, he may have been a target himself."

Reed stepped forward. "We object to introducing new suspects without full context—"

Judge Morgan cut him off. "You can respond in writing. For now, the court will accept both items as provisional exhibits, subject to review as I already stated."

Todd nodded once and returned to his seat. Adam

glanced over at him, eyes wide, as if for the first time in weeks he had a reason to believe this might end differently. Todd looked back at Rick, and Rick could see he was pleased that the judge had quickly shut down the prosecutor. Rick glanced over at the prosecutor, and steam was coming out of his ears. He knew he had underestimated Todd and had a tough fight ahead. Judge Matthew Morgan looked down at the prosecution table.

"Mr. Reed, you may proceed with your opening statement."

"Thank you, Your Honor."

David Reed buttoned his suit jacket as he stood. The courtroom was still, every eye turning toward him. He strolled to the center of the floor, paused, then turned to face the jury.

"Good morning," he began, his voice steady and measured. "Over the next several days, you'll hear a lot. Witnesses. Evidence. Arguments. But today, I want to give you a clear picture of this case."

He took a short breath, glancing briefly at Adam Olsen, who was sitting at the defendant's table, hands folded, his face unreadable.

"This case is about the murder of Paul Strasberg. And the man who killed him—Adam Olsen."

A murmur rippled through the gallery. Reed didn't flinch.

"On the morning of April 18th, Paul Strasberg was found dead and frozen in a box freezer on the set of a zombie movie out at the Bayou Sauvage National Wildlife Refuge. He had been almost decapitated by a stainless-steel ligature and disemboweled. There was a large bite mark on his face. But the ligature—the murder weapon—was found in a dumpster behind the hotel where the defendant was staying. And on that ligature, we found DNA. One belonged to the victim. The other belonged to Adam Olsen."

Reed let the words hang for a moment before continuing.

"That alone might raise questions. Maybe there's another explanation, right? Maybe he touched the ligature earlier, maybe it was a prop for the set. But there's more. We recovered a duffle bag with the defendant's initials embroidered on it in that dumpster as well. On that bag, we found blood that matched Paul Strasberg's DNA."

He took a step closer to the jury box. Reed's tone never changed. No theatrics. Just facts. That was his style.

"This isn't guesswork. This isn't a case built on theories or speculation. The DNA. The duffle bag. The blood. The murder weapon. It all points in one direction."

He turned slightly, gesturing toward the defense table without looking at it.

"When all the evidence is laid out, it will be clear. Adam Olsen murdered Paul Strasberg."

He nodded once, then returned to his seat.

The judge looked over his glasses at the defense attorney. "Counselor?"

The courtroom held its breath. Todd, rose from his chair with confidence, steady on his feet. He adjusted his cuffs, walked to the front of the courtroom, and faced the jury.

"Ladies and gentlemen," he began, his voice calm, not theatrical but direct, "you just heard a story from the prosecution. A tight, simple story. DNA on a murder weapon. A bag in a dumpster. It's a compelling narrative, no doubt. But stories can be compelling and still be wrong."

He let that sit a moment, walking slowly along the jury box.

"My client, Adam Olsen, is not a murderer. He's not a violent man. He has no criminal record. He had no reason to kill Paul Strasberg—because he loved him. They were in a relationship. They lived together for nearly two years. They shared a home, a life, and plans for the future. Paul wasn't just a roommate or a friend. He was the man Adam intended to spend his life with."

Todd turned toward the bench briefly, then back to the jury.

"And yet here we are. The prosecution will show you evidence—evidence that, on the surface, looks damaging. But I'm going to show you something else: context. Motive. And most importantly, reasonable doubt."

He stepped closer now, his tone firming up.

"Adam Olsen was not the killer. He was another intended victim. What happened on April 17th wasn't a random act or a crime of passion. It was part of something larger—something darker. Two men who were connected to this case are now dead. One of them, a man named Jason Bagley, had ties to the movie and another figure whose name or should I say names, will come up in this trial—Bill Hicklin aka Friedrich Wagner. Bill, as he was known on the set was using a fake passport and on the same flight from Germany as Paul and Adam. Coincidence. I think not. Both Bill and Jason are now deceased. And we believe both had reasons to want Paul Strasberg silenced."

Todd paused for just a moment.

"Adam was pulled into something that had already been set in motion. He was framed. Evidence was planted. And he's now the only one left to take the fall."

He took a step back, lowering his voice slightly.

"The prosecution will try to keep this case narrow and neat. But the truth rarely fits inside a clean box. The truth, in this case, is messier—and more dangerous. By the end of this trial, you'll see that Adam Olsen didn't murder Paul Strasberg. He lost him. And now he's being forced to fight for his own life in the wake of it."

He looked each juror in the eye, one by one, before returning to his seat beside his client.

The judge gave a slight nod. "Thank you, Mr. Thomas. Prosecution may call its first witness."

David stood. "The People call Alex Smith."

The courtroom doors opened, and a young man entered. Alex Smith looked nervous—early twenties, wearing a slightly wrinkled shirt and khakis. He walked to the witness stand and sat down after being sworn in by the bailiff.

The prosecutor approached.

"Please state your name and occupation for the record."

"Alex Smith. I'm a production assistant. I was working on a film called Voodoo Swamp."

"What kind of work did you do on that set?" asked David.

"Mostly errands—moving equipment, helping with props, making sure people were where they were supposed to be."

"Were you working on the morning of April 18th?"

"Yes."

"Tell the court what happened that morning."

Alex shifted in his seat. "I went to pull some animal entrails from one of the box freezers that we use as props for human guys in the zombie flesh-eating scenes. I pulled a few guts out, placed them in a sterile plastic bag, and that's when I saw a head. I thought it was just another prop at first, but when I tried to move it out of the way, I realized it was real and it was connected to a body. The body of Paul Strasberg, the assistant director."

Reed nodded. "What condition was he in?"

"He was well... dead. Frozen, not completely but partially, I'd say. He wasn't moving, of course. His lips were blue. He had a huge gash on his throat and a bite was taken out of his face. That's why at first, I thought it was a prop. I knew right away he was dead."

"What did you do next?"

"I ran out and yelled for help. Another crew member called 911. The police arrived soon after."

"Did you see Paul the night before?"

"Yes, left around 6:00 p.m. I think. Everyone thought he'd gone home."

Reed paused, then asked, "Was the freezer normally locked?"

"Yes. It had a latch on the outside, but also a safety handle on the inside so you could get out."

"Could he have gotten out on his own?"

"No. I suppose so, if he wasn't dead."

A quiet chuckle was heard through the courtroom. Judge Morgan raised a hand.

"Order."

Reed turned back to the witness.

"No further questions, Your Honor."

The judge turned to the defense table.

"Mr. Thomas, your witness."

Todd Thomas stood slowly and walked toward the stand. The courtroom waited.

"Hi Alex."

"Hi, sir."

"You can call me, Todd." he said, trying to relax the young guy.

"How long have you worked on this movie, Alex?"

"Since the beginning, before the new production company took over after the last one went on strike. I'm not a part of SAG, so I wasn't a part of the strike," said Alex.

"Can you tell the court what SAG is?"

"Sure. It stands for Screen Actors Guild. Screen Actors Guild-AFTRA to be precise. It's mainly for actors, but when actors go on strike, the production company usually stops production to stand in solidarity with the actors. That's why the German production company took over. That's where Paul came from. I'm not part of the union, so I can work anytime."

"I see. The night before you found Paul, do you remember the last time you saw him?" asked Todd.

"I think around 5:30 p.m. As I said, I left at 6:00 p.m."

"Who else do you remember seeing on the set? I know you wrapped that day around 5:00 p.m., correct?"

"Yeah, unless we are shooting night scenes. Possum, the new director likes to end the day at five. I remember seeing

Adam and a few extras hanging around, which wasn't unusual."

"Your Honor, I'd like to show Exhibits 9C and 9D to the witness."

The judge nodded, and Todd showed two 8x10 photos of Bill Hicklin, aka Friedrich Wagner and Jason Bagley to Alex.

"Do you remember seeing either or both of these guys on the set that day?"

Alex studied the photos.

"Yes, I saw them talking by the water cooler," said Alex.

"Did they look like they were conspiring to do something?"

"Objection, Your Honor, speculation."

"Sustained," replied the judge. "Disregard that question."

"I'm sorry, Your Honor. Let me rephrase that," said Todd.

"Since they were talking, they must know each other."

"Objection, speculation again," said David.

"Overruled, you may answer the question," said the judge.

"Yeah, they knew each other. Everyone knew everybody on the set. It's a small set," said Alex.

"No further questions, Your Honor," said Todd.

"You may step down, Mr. Smith," said Judge Morgan.

"Your Honor, I'd like to call my next witness."

"Proceed."

"The state calls Rick Waters to the stand."

Rick was in shock. He thought he might be called at some point, but not this soon in the trial. Todd was surprised too and rummaged through his notes as Rick placed his hand on the Bible and was sworn in.

"Mr. Waters, what do you do for a living?" asked prosecutor David Reed.

"What don't I do?" replied Rick with a smirk.

"Please answer the question, Mr. Waters. You are under oath."

"Okay. I own a charter boat company and private detective agency in Destin, Florida. I am a treasure finder, pool shark, part time craps gambler. I have an interest in a coffee, marijuana and house plant farm in Mississippi. I also track people, you know, like the show *Tracker* on CBS. Like I said, what don't I do? Rick crossed his arms.

"You said, treasure finder. Do you mean treasure hunter?"

"No finder, because I find things. Also, I apologize. I misspoke, I'm a part time craps winner, not gambler. Gamblers lose," said Rick.

"You think quite highly of yourself, don't you Mr. Waters?" asked Reed.

"Objection, Badgering the witness!" exclaimed Todd.

"I'll withdraw," said Todd.

"I'll answer the question if I may, Your Honor. I believe Mr. Reed is trying to show what kind of character I have."

The judge gave a knowing nod. "Go ahead."

"When you asked if I think highly of myself, I assume you meant, do I think I'm all that? Cocky and arrogant. That, I'm not. I'm just confident in my abilities. For instance, if you and I were to get into a fight, I'd kick your ass rather quickly," said Rick.

"Mr. Waters, I won't allow that kind of talk in my courtroom. Do you understand?" asked the judge.

"I'm sorry, Your Honor. He's being a dick."

The judge exhaled loudly.

"Last warning Mr. Waters or I will hold you in contempt."

Rick held up both hands, making a stopping gesture, then pretended to lock his mouth and throw away the key behind him. He could see that the prosecutor was bothered and upset, but he liked that just fine.

"Mr. Waters, you say you are a private detective. Have you been investigating this case?"

"I have."

"Don't you think that's a conflict of interest?"

"In what way?" asked Rick.

"Aren't you the custodial guard of the accused?"

"Yes, he's with me 24/7. I don't see how that's a conflict of interest. I'm sure you have a daughter or son. When they were younger, if they did something wrong or were accused of something wrong, did you not look into it? Same thing."

It was clear that Reed was completely flustered and ready to ring Rick's neck.

"No further questions, Your Honor," said Reed.

"Your witness, counsel," the judge said to Todd.

"No questions at this time, Your Honor."

Rick stepped down and assumed his seat in the second row. Todd looked back at him and shook his head. Todd regrouped himself. He wasn't sure why Rick was so aggressive toward the prosecutor, but he would find out once the judge called recess. It was time for Todd to start planting reasonable doubt.

"Your Honor, if the state will allow, I'd like to call an

expert witness to the stand. He has to fly back to Chicago soon. He is on the witness list. I'd like to call him now, so he can return home, if the state doesn't object to him being called out of order."

The judge looked at the prosecutor, nodded for a go-ahead, and said,

"No objection, Your Honor."

The defense summoned Dr. Alan Schwartz to the stand."

A heavyset, balding man approached the witness stand, took an oath, and sat down. Todd casually walked over to him and glanced back at Adam. He asked the judge for permission to set up a large aluminum easel with some enlarged photos on transparent plastic next to the jury box. The bailiff brought them out, and they were recorded with their exhibit numbers.

"Dr. Schwartz, what is your occupation?" asked Todd.

"I am a forensic odontologist."

"Whoa, that's a big word. Can you break it down into bite-sized pieces for me? Forgive the pun. I'm sure the jury understands what a forensic odontologist is, but I'm a little thick," said Todd.

Several jurors laughed when he said that. Todd was exceptionally charming as a defense attorney.

"It means I'm a tooth and bite mark expert, basically," he said.

"Oh, I get it. So, it's possible to match the bite marks of something to photos or a cast from a suspect? It can be used in court?" asked Todd.

"That's how they nailed Ted Bundy."

"Wow, that's right. I remember that. They had to get a

warrant to get him to give a cast because he knew it would be the nail in his coffin and it was," replied Todd.

"Okay, so I'd like you and the jury to look at this first photo. I know it's a bit gruesome. What is this a photo of?" asked Todd.

Dr Schwartz looked at the photo.

"That is a photo of the bite mark on Paul Strasberg's right cheek."

"Can everyone see that?" asked Todd.

The jury nodded and some murmured yes.

"What is unique about that photo, Dr Schwartz?"

"You can clearly see that whoever bit Mr. Strasberg in the cheek is missing a lateral incisor. Whoever bit him has a big gap where that tooth should be," he said.

"So, if that person was to smile like my client, you'd see the gap?" asked Todd as he pointed over to Adam.

Adam gave a big smile and held it.

The jury gasped, and several jurors exchanged glances.

"That's correct. It would be as obvious as the nose on your face," said Dr. Schwartz.

"No further questions, Your Honor."

"Your witness, counsel," said the judge as he looked at Reed.

"Dr. Schwartz, isn't odontology for court cases nothing more than junk science?"

"I beg your pardon," said Dr. Schwartz.

"If it pleases the court, I'd like to read an excerpt from an article from The Guardian magazine. Charles McCrory is haunted by a memory from his 1985 trial in which he was accused of murdering his wife, Julie Bonds, in a bloody attack at their home in Andalusia, a small town in deepest Alabama.

What haunts him is the look on the jurors' faces as they listened to the testimony of the prosecution's star witness, a dentist named Richard Souviron. He was a founding father of a cutting-edge branch of forensic science known as bite-mark analysis, which claimed to be able to identify violent criminals by matching their unique dental patterns to the bite wounds on victims' bodies.

McCrory was expecting Souviron's evidence to be nuanced. In his initial report, the dentist had been cautious about what could be deduced from two puncture marks found on the upper right arm of Julie's body, saying that the injuries were insufficiently distinct to allow a positive match with the perpetrator.

But that was not what he told the jury.

When Souviron was asked whether the two marks were teeth marks, he said: "Yes."

Then the prosecutor asked him: "In your expert opinion, based on the evidence presented to you, were these teeth marks made by Charles McCrory?"

"Yes," the dentist replied.

McCrory remembers vividly the sinking feeling he experienced in that moment, given the glaring contrast between Souviron's initial report and what he was now saying in court. "I was in disbelief at his testimony being so different," he recalled. "I knew it was extremely damaging to our case. You could see it in the eyes of the jurors."

Reed paused and turned to the jury.

What you didn't read is that Charles McCrory spent

twenty-four years behind bars based on the testimony of one word. YES. When asked if Mr. McCrory left that bite mark on his wife, the so-called expert witness said YES. Did you also know that Mr. McCrory's case was overturned and he was released as a free man after the so-called expert witness recanted his testimony and said he had no way of knowing if McCrory left that bite mark on his wife or if it was even a bite mark at all?"

Reed slammed his palm against the jury box railing, startling some of the jurors.

"Twenty-four years! He spent twenty-four years behind bars because of junk science. I have no further questions."

Reed walked back to his table with his back to the jury and winked at Todd. Todd bit his lip. That was a significant blow to the defense. Since the bite mark wasn't tested for DNA and Paul's body was already cremated, Todd had to put it behind him and move on. He knew Adam hadn't bitten Paul, but he also knew the jury would have doubts about whether the evidence was solid. He had to hand it to Reed. He won that battle, but the war was far from over.

CHAPTER

FIFTEEN

Rick texted Todd with part of the PDF he had just received from the coroner's office in Tammany Parish. Thallium was found in Bill Hicklin's blood. Now, not only were two extras on the set of the movie affected, but both men were poisoned with thallium. Todd asked the judge if he could approach the bench.

"Your Honor, I have just received evidence that shows the second deceased man on the set of the movie, where the victim worked as assistant director, had thallium in his blood, which was the cause of death. I'd like to enter that into evidence. There's no way that was a coincidence."

"I agree, Mr. Thomas. Bailiff, please index the new evidence for the prosecution."

Todd returned to his seat at the prosecution table. Jules, Possum, and Gary sat in the gallery and watched. Filming that day had been paused since all their names were on the witness list, and any or all of them could be called to testify. Possum had been editing the movie they filmed in Egypt while also directing the new film. He had been working sixteen-hour days, and being away from the set was a welcome break.

"Your Honor, I'd like to call Michael Jackson to the stand," said Reed.

There was a gasp and a shocked look when he said that. Possum stood up, proceeded to the witness stand, and was sworn in. Several jurors shot glances at each other as he approached.

"Good morning. Your name is Michael Jackson? That must have been an odd thing to grow up with."

"It's actually Thomas Michael Jackson, but my friends call me Possum."

Reed flipped through his notes.

"Ah, my mistake. I meant Thomas Michael Jackson. But Possum? That's quite an odd nickname, too. How did that come about?"

"Objection." said Todd, "Irrelevant."

"I'll allow it. Proceed, Mr. Reed."

"You can answer the question, Possum. Is that okay if I call you that?" asked Reed.

"Sure. I've always loved the music of George Jones, whose nickname was The Possum. One day in high school, someone called me Possum while I was listening to one of Jones' albums. The name just stuck."

"I see, Mr. Possum," said Reed.

"It's just Possum."

"My apologies, *Possum*. You worked closely with Paul

Strasberg on the set here in Louisiana as well as in Egypt. Is that correct?"

"It is."

"So, is it safe to say you got to know him quite well?"

"Yeah, we worked together a lot; he had a great eye for camera angles."

"What kind of man would you say he was? Can you give us a quick rundown?" asked Reed.

"He was quiet, calculated, and a consummate professional. I am new to filmmaking, so I leaned on him for advice often."

"Would you call him a stand-up guy? Trustworthy?"

"Yeah, I'd say so. I only knew him from work. He did come to a few dinners with us in Egypt."

"You knew he was gay. Did that bother you?"

"I could care less. I'm straight, but his life choices didn't affect his work on set, and it was none of my business. My philosophy is live and let live," said Possum.

"Were you aware that he was in a relationship with the defendant?"

"Of course. Adam was on the set often. Everyone knew. It never caused an issue while filming and Adam never argued or got in the way. He always stayed behind the cameras and was a complete gentleman. I think Paul enjoyed having him come to the set. It's nice when you can spend time with your partner at work during breaks, lunch, and whatnot," said Possum.

"Did you see Adam speaking to either of the deceased extras on the set ever?" asked Reed.

"Nothing springs to mind. I was focused on filmmaking.

Extras often hung out between takes and chatted. It wasn't exactly something I paid attention to. It's a small set. People get bored."

"So would you say the defendant might have spent time talking to the two men?"

"Anything's possible," replied Possum.

"No further questions, Your Honor," said Reed.

The judge stretched his neck and then glanced over at Todd.

"Your witness, Mr. Thomas."

"Good morning, Possum."

"Good morning."

"I'd like to take you back to the night Paul was murdered. You were on the set that night, correct? I know, according to Rick, that you stayed after hours on many nights and worked in the editing trailer on your last film."

"Yes, I often stayed late and slept in the editing trailer. But that night, we wrapped early and I went to dinner with Rick, and the gang in New Orleans."

"Do you recall the restaurant you ate at?" asked Todd.

"Of course. We got a private dining room at Cochon's," said Possum.

"Why a private dining room?"

"It was for a celebration. Rick snuck off and got married in Nashville without telling us and wanted to let us all know about it and have a little party, so to speak."

"Do you remember who all was there?" asked Todd.

"Let me think. There was Rick and Jules, myself of course, Gary, Johnie and Clay. So the five of us."

"Why wasn't Paul invited? I know you testified that he had gone to dinners with you before while filming in Egypt."

"Rick told Gary he only wanted the five of us and none of the crew. It was personal."

"I understand. Do you remember what time you left the set?" asked Todd.

"Gary and I left early. About 4:30 p.m. Gary wanted to make sure the private room was set up, so he and I went to Cochon's, checked on the table, then walked across the street to the Ugly Dog Saloon and had a couple of drinks while we waited for the rest of the guys to show up."

"Paul was still on the set when you left?"

"Yes."

"What about Adam?"

Possum looked up at the ceiling, trying to remember.

"To be honest, I don't remember seeing Adam, when I left."

"So, he may have already left the set?"

"Objection, speculation!" exclaimed Reed.

"Your Honor, I'm just trying to establish the whereabouts of my client the day Paul was murdered."

"It's quite easy to figure that out. You should have a printout of all the crew and extras. There was a little trouble on the set before I took over as director. A group of animal rights protestors had invaded the set, and there was some vandalism and violence. Since Gary is a major investor and producer, he felt it was better to hire security and close the set to visitors. Only approved actors, extras, and crew were allowed on the set and had to show ID coming and going. I believe his insurance required it," said Possum.

Todd returned to the prosecution table and picked up a piece of paper.

"I have the copy here of the log sheet for that day. It's exhibit number 11c, Your Honor."

"Noted," replied the judge.

Todd handed Possum the log sheet.

"Can you scroll down the list and find Adam Olsen's name and read that to the court?"

Possum ran his finger down the list and saw Paul and Adam's names signed up next to each other.

"It shows Adam's name checking in at 8:10 a.m., right below Paul's name."

"Does it show Adam signing out?"

"Yes, it shows he left the set at 3:40 p.m."

"I also have an eyewitness from the front desk who has him getting some fresh towels at 4:05 p.m. What time does it show Paul left that day?"

"It's blank. That's the night he was murdered. Paul stayed late: he told me he was going to shoot some b-roll of the zombies walking around," said Possum.

"So, there were quite a few extras still on the set when you left?"

"Yeah, I'd say the majority of them."

"Can you scroll down that list and tell me who the last person to sign out was?"

Possum ran his finger up and down the list and then stopped and paused.

"The last person to sign out was Bill Hicklin."

"What time was that?"

"8:47 p.m."

"How about the last person before him?" asked Todd.

Once again, Possum scrolled up and down the list.

"Several other extras signed out at around 7:15 p.m. I don't know all their names by heart, but I remember Paul saying he was gonna wrap for the day about seven."

"Do you find it off that Bill Hicklin signed out almost an hour and a half later than everyone else?" asked Todd.

"Yes, I do."

"You said you have security on the set. Do they stay there 24/7?"

"We have like five or six security guards on the set while filming, and there's always one that stays all night. They rotate. There's only one way in and out of the refuge where the set is," said Possum.

"According to what you are saying, Paul never signed out. My client, Adam Olsen, signed out at 3:40 p.m., Bill signed out at 8:47 p.m., and no one signed back in that night."

"That's correct."

"I have no further questions, Your Honor."

Possum stepped down and sat beside Rick.

"Rick, there's no way Adam did this; he was at the hotel from 4:05 p.m. on. His alibi is rock solid. He was framed," whispered Possum.

"I know, buddy. We need more evidence to prove he was drugged and framed. The hotel surveillance shows him checking in and getting the towels. If we could prove that someone put the GHB in his drink, it would seal the deal."

"Were there cameras in the gym?" asked Possum.

"Yes, but they are automatically erased every twenty-four hours at 8:00 a.m. Adam said someone came in wearing black sweatpants and hoodie. I think that's the killer and the one who drugged his Under Armor cup. I'd bet my last dollar that it was Jason Bagley. He's the only one with motive. He's a crazy animal rights activist. It fits."

"Do you know if the camera in the gym is on a hard drive or on the cloud?"

"Would assume a hard drive, but I'm not certain. Why?" asked Rick.

"I have an idea. I'm going to the hotel."

Possum bumped fists with Rick and proceeded out of the courtroom. He borrowed the keys for the rental car from Gary, who had to stay in case he was called up to testify. He called the hotel posing as a computer repair tech.

"Hi, may I speak to the manager?"

A few moments passed, and someone picked up the phone.

"Dis is Sherrie, de manager. How may I help you?"

"Hi Sherrie. I got call from corporate and they asked me to do a routine service on the security hard drives in your location. We service all brands of security systems. Can you do me a favor, darlin'? Can you go into the room where the hard drives are stored and tell me what brand your hotel uses? It'll save me a trip in case I need to replace any parts on them."

"Sure thing, hun. Hang in a minute."

A few moments went by, and she returned to the phone.

"It says Lorex Pro on de cover."

"You are a sweetheart. I'll be heading your way shortly."

He went to the Lorex Pro website and researched which replacement hard drives were compatible with the units at the hotel. It turned out they used standard 3.5" SATA hard disk drives. He drove to the nearest Best Buy, bought four hard drives and some empty hard drive enclosures, along with a computer repair toolkit. He stopped at Walmart and bought some blue coveralls and a small leather tool bag. After placing the toolkit and the new hard drives in the bag, he headed to the hotel. Once he arrived, he met with the manager, who showed him the room where they kept the hard drives. He introduced himself as Michael from AAA Security Company and explained that the entire security system was under a maintenance contract from corporate.

"Where are all the cameras?" he asked.

"We have one at each end of de halls, one at de entrance, one in de gym, and a few in de parking lot. Oh, and one in de back by de dumpsters. I believe dat's it," she said.

"It might be while," said Possum.

"No problem, honey. Take yo time. I'm here all night," she said as she walked back to the front desk and disappeared into her office.

Possum stepped into the hard drive room and got to work. One by one, he removed the covers from the hard drives, carefully unplugged them from the motherboard, and replaced them with the blank ones he had just purchased from Best Buy. It took him about an hour to swap out all the hard drives. He thanked the manager and headed to the set. His MacBook was in the editing trailer. After installing all the hard drives from the hotel into the new enclosures, he hooked up his MacBook to the first one and opened a program he had that searched for lost data.

When a hard drive is erased, it's not completely erased.

The data remains hidden in layers and can be retrieved. This phenomenon is known as data remanence. The SATA SSD drive that the hotel used could store remanent data for as long as seventy years or longer. The detectives on the case may or may not have known that, but once they were informed that the drives had been erased, they didn't even bother because they were so focused on Adam being the killer that they didn't care. The hard drives were scheduled to overwrite the recordings daily at 8:00 a.m. unless they were manually stopped, such as if an incident occurred and they needed to make a copy of it. The video data remained on the hard drive, compressed and hidden in layers. The program Possum used would recover the hidden data, but it took a lot of time. He programmed it to find the date Paul was killed and set it to capture everything from noon that day until the next morning, when Adam was discovered sleeping on a lounge chair at the pool.

Possum had to do each hard drive individually. He copied all of the recovered data to a two-terabyte external hard drive he already owned and created a folder on it for each hard drive. While the program ran on his MacBook, he fired up the AVID editing system, made a pot of coffee and settled in for the night.

Rick, Jules, Gary, and Adam left the courtroom bound for Todd's office. Todd and Anthony were waiting for them when they arrived.

"First things first. Why did you give the prosecutor so much shit yesterday. I didn't have a chance to ask you yet."

"Two reasons. One, I wanted to rattle his cage a little and two, he was dick," said Rick.

"I'll give you that much. I guess it didn't cause any damage. I mean, you're not a suspect, and you ain't on trial. As a matter of fact, I did see him getting upset, which means his emotions might get the best of him. That was pretty clever, comparing your situation to his own kids when he brought up the conflict-of-interest question," said Todd.

"Why, thank you, kind sir."

"We are sitting pretty good so far. The prosecutor scored some points with the junk science attack against our tooth molds and images. The case he was referring to, though, involved just two small impressions, not a complete removal of flesh from a body like we have. We know Adam couldn't have done that. Look at his teeth! He has a perfectly straight smile. But I don't want to confuse the jury any further, so I'm gonna leave it alone. I'm going to focus hard on Adam being framed and alternative suspects."

"That log sheet showing Adam signing out was gold! Possum thought so too, and he went to the hotel to try and recover the remanent data from the hard drives," said Rick.

"The hard drives need to be removed to do that procedure. We'll need a warrant," said Todd.

"We don't need no stinking warrants. Possum will handle it," said Rick with a grin.

"I don't want to know anything about it!" exclaimed Todd.

"What's the plan for tomorrow?" asked Rick.

"I'm going to call up some witnesses to build up Adam's credibility as a person. Rick, you and Jules have gotten to know him the most so I will probably call you up, but I have some great news. Adam, I managed to talk your mother into testifying about you. She's landing tonight. Would you like to pick her up with Rick, or do you want me to get her and bring her to the hotel?"

"Oh my God, really? But she doesn't even have a passport," said Adam.

"She does now. I wanted to surprise you but since she's coming tonight, I thought I'd go ahead and tell you," said Todd.

"It is customary in our country to give gifts when we receive a visitor. Nothing huge, just something convenient. If it's okay, Todd, can you pick her up and bring her to the hotel? Rick, would you mind stopping somewhere on the way back so I can pick up some flowers for her and a little something? What time does she land?" asked Adam.

"She arrives at 7:15 p.m., said Todd."

"We can stop wherever you like on the way back, Todd," added Rick.

"I'm so excited. I haven't seen her in over two years. I wish it were under different circumstances," said Adam.

"Do you want me to book her a room, or do you want her to stay in yours?" asked Rick.

"Definitely mine. She can have the bed, and I'll use the pull-out from the couch."

Once the meeting wrapped up, Rick stopped at a little gift shop called Forever New Orleans on Royal Street, and Adam picked up a local book, a small porcelain owl and a gift bag. They stopped off at Rouses Market, and he bought her a nice flower arrangement as well.

"She's been into owls for as long as I remember," said Adam as they arrived at the hotel.

He was giddy to see his mom and couldn't hide his excitement.

"I tell you what, Adam. Once she arrives, after we meet her, why don't you order room service so that the two of you can eat in your room and visit? Jules and I will probably step out to the Creole House. I trust you and know you ain't going anywhere," said Rick.

"Thank you, Rick. That means a lot."

CHAPTER

SIXTEEN

R ick was sipping coffee when Possum called.

"Hey, Amigo. I have good news and bad news. What do you want first?"

"The good news."

"The software is working, and I should be able to retrieve all the video from the cameras the day Paul was murdered."

"What's the bad news?" Rick asked reluctantly.

"I'm only three-quarters of the way through the first hard drive, and the software ran all night. It's gonna take forever."

"Damn, there's no way to speed that up?"

"I'm afraid not."

"We have a corroborating witness that says Adam took some towels from the front desk. So maybe you can skip the lobby hard drive and focus on the gym, pool, and are there any cameras facing the dumpsters?"

"Great minds think alike, buddy. The first hard drive I'm working on is the gym. It also contains videos from the pool. When I looked at the live feed, I could see that the camera captures the bench press and the row of treadmills. If we're lucky, we will see his face when he enters the gym from the pool area. The feed to the pool has a clear shot of the lounge chair where Adam went unconscious. I should be able to finish that drive today, and I'll immediately start the one facing the dumpsters. I wish I had a second MacBook; I could do two at a time," said Possum.

"Use mine, dummy. It's in the motorhome. I'll text you the password."

"Duh. I don't know why I didn't think of that! It'll save time."

Rick and Jules took Adam and his mother to the courthouse. It was a madhouse with cameras everywhere. Mrs. Olsen was quite upset and nervous when she entered the courtroom. Jules held her hand, comforted her, and assured her that everything would be okay.

Once the judge arrived and everyone was seated, the prosecutor called his first witness. He called a few extras from the movie set but didn't gain much ground. Todd didn't cross-examine any of them because they didn't offer anything to the case, and Reed didn't score any victories.

"Your Honor, I'd like to call to the stand Mrs. Freja Olsen."

Mrs. Olsen was sworn in and sat down at the witness stand.

"Hello, Mrs. Olsen. Thank you for making the long trip from Denmark to be here," said Todd.

"My pleasure, Mr. Thomas."

"This is your first trip abroad, is it not?"

"That's correct. Anything for my son."

"Can you tell me about Adam. What kind of boy was he growing up?"

"Adam was a good boy. He did well in school and got high marks. He attended university and got his PhD in Chemistry," she said.

"You must be extremely proud of him."

"Oh yes. He could've gone to work for any Big Pharma company in the world but chose to follow his dream to become a professional trainer and eventually create his own line of health supplements. He was recruited heavily by Novo Nordisk but turned it down," she said.

"That's incredible. I'm sure he would've been paid a nice salary there."

"Yes, it would've been. But fitness is his life and his passion," she said.

"Did Adam ever get into any trouble as an adult?"

"Never. He has always been a law-abiding citizen. I know he didn't do this. A mother knows her son, and Adam couldn't hurt a fly."

"Thank you, Mrs. Olsen. That is all I have for now."

"Your witness, counselor," said the judge as he glanced over at the prosecution table.

David Reed scoured through his notes for a moment before standing up and approaching Mrs. Olsen.

"Mrs. Olsen. You say you know your son, but do you really? I assume you know he is gay?"

"Of course. What does that have to do with anything?"

"Nothing really, but did you know he had several lovers at the same time when he started dating Paul, the victim?"

"No. I don't butt into his love life. As long as he is happy, that is all that I care about," she said.

"It doesn't bother you that he had multiple partners?"

"Objection, badgering the witness. She already said she doesn't butt into his love life, Your Honor," said Todd.

"Sustained," replied the judge.

Todd could see some frowns from the jurors, suggesting that Reed's line of questioning had offended some of them. Anyone in their right mind could see how much Mrs. Olsen loved her son.

"No more questions, Your Honor."

The trial continued, and the next few days felt like Groundhog Day. One day, the prosecution would score a few points, and the next day, the defense would win the battle. It was hard to tell who was ahead. It felt like one of those football games where both teams were evenly matched, and whoever had the ball last would win. Todd hoped he was wrong because, in criminal cases, the prosecution gets the final word to the jury in closing arguments.

Possum called a meeting, and everyone except Gary gathered at Todd's office. Gary had dinner plans and wasn't needed. Possum requested Todd to set up a flat-screen TV with an HDMI cable to connect to his MacBook.

"Okay, it took a while, but it was worth it. I think I found our smoking gun. Watch this," said Possum.

He first mentioned the gym's video surveillance, which clearly displayed the bench press area. You could just make out the top half of Adam's Under Armor insulated bottle. After completing his bench press sets, he set the cup down and went to the bathroom. A minute and a half later, a man wearing a black sweatsuit and hoodie limped in through the door leading from the pool. The door to the pool and the door to the bathrooms were situated side by side at an angle but the bathroom door was just out of view because it was on a different wall. The man wore large sunglasses, and his hoodie was pulled tight. Unfortunately, there was no way to identify his face, but he had a similar build to Jason Bagley.

After walking just a few steps, he glanced back, then quickly unscrewed Adam's cup, poured something into it, screwed it back on, and carefully placed it in the exact same position, facing the same direction. He quickly exited the gym through the pool door. A couple of minutes later Adam returned from the bathroom, sat down on the bench press seat and took a big swig from the Under Armor bottle. He walked over to the kettlebells and picked up two twenty-pounders. He did both workouts like he had stated before, then stepped out of the door to the pool.

"Did you notice he was limping?" asked Possum as he switched to the pool camera.

The pool camera was positioned directly above the door leading from the gym and had a clear view of the lounge chair where Adam eventually succumbed to the GHB. The chair was on the far side of the pool, and once Adam was about halfway across the pool deck, he appeared on camera. He wasn't carrying his bottle, and he didn't have his gym bag with him. He looked a bit unsteady and plopped down on the edge of the lounge chair. In less than thirty seconds, he fell backward, and his arms flopped to the concrete. He lay motionless, half on and half off the lounge chair. Possum fast-forwarded the video, and according to the timestamp, Adam remained in that position on camera for the next eight and a half hours. His story was checking out.

"What about the cameras facing the dumpsters?" asked Rick.

"I'm getting there; hold your horses."

Possum switched to a different file. The same man wearing the black tracksuit limped into view carrying a paper grocery bag in one hand and Adam's Under Armor duffel bag in the other. He tossed the duffel bag into the dumpster, then turned the grocery bag upside down, causing the ligature to fall into the dumpster.

"Boom!" exclaimed Possum. "We now have definitive proof that Adam was framed. Since we never see the man's face, we can't prove who he is, but we can plant reasonable doubt that it might be Jason Bagley. The size and height are matches. Plus, Jason had a stiff knee according to the file we have on him when he auditioned to be an extra. Look at this. The casting director notes it."

They all leaned closer to see the paper Possum took out of a manila folder.

Under Jason Bagley's name and photo, it read: hair color – brown, height - 5' 11", weight – 205 lbs. Then in parentheses, it said (has bad left knee and walks with a limp, perfect for a zombie extra).

"That's it! I will introduce this to the judge in the morning. Any other judge would most likely dismiss this case immediately without prejudice, and that's a possibility, but this judge is corrupt and loves the spotlight. He might want to finish out the trial for more camera time on the local news. Rumor has it that he is considering a run for Louisiana State District Attorney. That's quite a step up from Orleans Parish judge. And as they say, any publicity is good publicity," said Todd.

"Can you play that last video again, where the man comes into view from the left side of the camera and throws away the evidence?" asked Rick.

Possum rewound the video and played it again. It was evident the man had a bad left knee. Rick picked up the file from the casting director.

"It even says left knee. It gives me an idea. I'm going to talk to Mrs. Bagley. Do you guys need me anymore? Possum, can you take Adam to the hotel once y'all are done? Jules, you wanna take a ride?"

Possum nodded, and Jules picked up her purse and followed Rick to the Jeep. Rick drove over to Mrs. Bagley's house in Gretna. They stepped down from the Jeep, and Rick knocked on the door. A few minutes later, she came to the door.

"Well, hello, Mr. and Mrs. Waters. What brings you here tonight? Come in, come in, please."

Jules didn't correct her, even though Jules' last name was still Castro. Rick and Jules sat down on the couch, and Mrs. Bagley sat in her La-Z-Boy.

"Oh, heavens me, forgive my manners. Can I get you two something to drink?"

They both declined.

"Mrs. Bagley, the reason I am here is that I wanted to ask you about Jason. Did he always walk with a limp?"

"No, no, it's been about five years since his accident," she said.

"Accident?" asked Rick.

"Oh yes. He was injured at work. He worked at Manley Steel. He and another man were stacking some steel girders in the warehouse, and I guess the man who was helping wasn't paying attention and stacked them too high. The entire stack fell, and one of the girders hit Jason in the leg. He had to go to the hospital. They performed several surgeries on him, and he received a knee replacement and a metal rod in his leg. His left leg was broken in several places. He never walked the same after that. He sued the company and won. I'm not supposed to tell you how much, but he never worked again and just pursued hobbies and the occasional side gig, like being an extra in films. He traveled a lot with the money, mostly to Europe. Germany, I think. I believe he met someone there, but I never met him," she said.

"Would you testify about his limp and injury in court?" asked Rick.

"Of course. I did it once; I can do it again. Wait...I can do better than that. When Jason's lawyer was building the lawsuit against the company, he had me film Jason walking to show his mobility. I have the DVD in a file with the rest of his court papers. He had me keep it all here for him because he didn't have a safe, and I do. Hold on a minute."

She stepped out of the living room and returned a few minutes later with an accordion-style folder and handed it to Rick.

"You can't show anyone the amount of money he won, but you can use the rest of it. Part of the settlement agreement was that he was not to discuss the amount," said Mrs. Bagley.

"Thank you so much, Mrs. Bagley. With all this, you may not have to appear again. I will let you know, okay?" asked Rick.

"I'll be there if you need me. Do you think this might help find out who killed my Jason?"

"Something like that," said Rick.

He didn't have the heart to tell her that it would likely shine a spotlight on Jason as Paul's killer. He hoped the video would be enough and that she wouldn't have to return to court. They left and drove straight back to the hotel. In their room was a DVD player connected to the main TV. Few people used it, but videos were available to borrow in the club-level lounge. Rick popped the DVD into the player and turned on the TV. In the video, Jason walked back and forth, side to side, in the same living room they had just left while Mrs. Bagley filmed him. You could hear her on the video telling him to turn around and walk the other way. It was the exact same limp they had just seen on the man in the surveillance video they had watched at Todd's office.

Rick wiped his hands together to imply he was washing his hands of the case, that it was over. Open and shut. He texted Todd the news and told him he'd hand over the file and the video in the morning before court. Todd said he would come over immediately and collect it. He had to make copies and give them to the prosecution as discovery, or they'd never be allowed at the trial.

A half an hour later, Todd arrived at Rick's room.

"Come on in," said Rick.

Todd stepped inside.

"You got a beer?" asked Todd. "This is huge."

"Yeah, I think there's some in the wet bar. You wanna see the DVD. It's still in the player," said Rick.

"Hell yeah!"

After holding up a beer for Todd to see, and after Todd nodded, Rick popped the top and handed him a bottle of Abita Andygator, a popular local beer brewed near Covington. Rick stepped over to the DVD player and pushed play. Todd watched as he sipped his beer.

"Holy smoking gun! That's it. That's the straw that will break the proverbial back of that smug camel Reed. It wouldn't surprise me if he asked the judge for a dismissal," said Todd.

Rick popped open the DVD and handed it along with the expandable folder to Todd.

"Thanks for the beer. I hate to drink and dash, but I need to make a copy of this. Possum and Adam are still at my office, and Possum is burning copies of the surveillance video for the prosecution. I have to give it to him tonight before I present it to the judge as evidence. He's easy to find—drinks every night at Barrel Proof in the Lower Garden District. I've met him there several times."

Todd thanked Rick again and returned to his office. When

he arrived, Possum had just finished making copies of the surveillance videos. Todd showed him the video Rick got from Mrs. Bagley, and he burned a DVD copy for him. Adam and Possum left, and Todd locked up his office. He drove over to Barrel Proof, and just as he thought, David Reed, the prosecutor, was sitting at his usual table, nursing a single malt scotch.

"David."

"Why hello, Todd. What brings you to my watering hole?"

Todd pulled up a chair as David called over the cocktail waiters.

"Scotch?"

"Why not," replied Todd.

They made small talk for a minute, and the waitress brought over Todd's drink. He took a sip.

"Mmm, mmm. Tastes like velvet," said Todd.

"Only the best counselor," replied David.

Todd placed his briefcase on the table, opened it, pulled out a DVD and a file folder, and slid it over to David.

"What's this?"

"Discovery. Or should I call it your demise? I will present this as new evidence to the judge in the morning. I suggest you finish your drink and watch it. You may want to consider dismissing all charges, but I'll leave that up to you. I know DAs hate to lose cases, so at least a dismissal won't sting so bad."

David raised his eyebrow in curiosity. Todd let him brew for a minute, finished his drink and stood up.

"Next one's on me after the trial."

Todd turned around and walked out of the bar with his head held high.

Once the judge sat down, David Reed, the people's prosecutor, asked to approach the bench. Todd also stood up and listened.

"Your Honor, the defense has given me discovery that sheds light on the case. I need more time to review it before I can proceed," said Reed.

"Both of you, in my chamber and bring the discovery," said the judge.

The three of them disappeared through a door behind the bench.

"What is this new discovery?" asked the judge.

Reed handed the judge the file folder and DVD

"You'll have to watch it, Your Honor," he said.

The judge popped open his DVD/TV player and stuck the DVD in the slot. He put his hand on his chin and watched. Once the entire video was finished, he ejected the DVD and handed it back to Reed.

"Counselor, that flips this case on its head. What would you like to do?"

"I'd like to request a three-day continuance, so I can review the evidence, and have it confirmed as authentic by an expert before I move forward," replied Reed.

"I'll give you two days starting today. We're not gonna let this linger over the weekend. Now return to your tables."

The judge returned to the bench and began to speak.

"Ladies and gentlemen, new potential exculpatory evidence has been introduced to this case. I have allowed a two-day continuance. The jury shall remain sequestered and is reminded to not discuss the case with anyone. We are now in recess until Friday."

The judge pounded his gavel, and everyone stood up and began exiting the courtroom.

CHAPTER
SEVENTEEN

Todd patted Adam on the back, looked back at Rick, and smiled. They all met in the hallway.

"Now what?" asked Rick.

"We wait. If things go the way I think they will, Friday should be a good day for us," said Todd.

Adam, Rick, and Jules walked to the Jeep, avoiding the press as best they could and ignoring any questions thrown at them.

"Who's hungry?"

"It's still early, but I'm peckish," said Jules.

"Why don't we go pick up your mother and Chief at the hotel and go to a place that has brunch seven days a week? My treat. It's a chain but it's damn good," said Rick.

They picked up Adam's mom and Chief, and Jules let her sit in the front seat with Rick while she held Chief in the backseat with Adam. Rick pulled into the parking lot of the Ruby Slipper in the Warehouse District, while Jules placed

Chief in his travel backpack, gave him some tongue depressors, and then cracked the windows. Since there was nothing to do for a few days and Possum had given the crew, actors, and extras a break until Monday, Rick thought it would be nice to show Adam's mom around New Orleans a bit.

Rick ordered peach and cream beignets for the whole table to start. Jules asked for a menu, but Rick, Adam, and Mrs. Olsen all chose to have the weekday brunch. After Jules looked at the menu for a while, she decided on the avocado toast with a side of scrambled eggs. Rick pigged out and kept asking for different items from the brunch menu. Jules gave him the evil eye then smiled. He was happy. It was apparent. She'd let him gorge himself on carbs, then kick his ass later in the gym.

After breakfast, Rick drove around New Orleans, showing Mrs. Olsen all the amazing architecture he was so fond of. They hit all the districts. He even drove out to the Ninth Ward and showed her the waterline still visible on some of the abandoned homes after Katrina. He took them to the old cemeteries and showed them the graves and mausoleums that sat above ground, explaining that the water table was so high that New Orleans was actually below the waterline and the only thing keeping it from flooding was the levees.

Once they had seen the best of New Orleans, Rick asked Mrs. Olsen if she had ever seen the Gulf or a beach. She explained that Denmark has many beaches and Amager Beach Park was only a fifteen-minute drive from where she lived in Copenhagen, but that she would love to see a beach in the U.S. Rick told her there was a really lovely white beach in Bay St. Louis a little over an hour away. They all agreed that the road trip would be worth it, and Jules reminded Rick about Cuz's Old Town Oyster Bar & Grill, which they had once dined at and loved.

When they arrived in Bay St. Louis, the afternoon sun was sitting in the sky casting a warm light on the white sand. They all piled out of the Jeep, and Mrs. Olsen took off her shoes and stepped on the sand.

"It's squeaky," she said.

"Yeah, it's kinda like the beaches in Destin, but the water in Destin is bluer because it has the Gulf Stream closer to shore and the town was further away from the muddy Mississippi River," explained Rick.

They spent a few hours walking on the beach, and both Jules and Mrs. Olsen collected shells. It gave Rick some time to talk to Adam alone.

"What are your plans, Adam, if the charges are dropped or you are acquitted?"

Adam picked up a shell and skipped it across the calm water.

"I'm not sure. I might talk to Gary about investing in my health supplements if you think he'd still be interested. Or I might move back to Denmark. Since Paul is gone, I feel kind of lost. I might just take some time off and move back in with my mom. You know, decompress before I make a big life-changing plan," said Adam.

"That's wise. I once read that after a tragedy or bad breakup, it's best to take a little time before making any big decisions. Sometimes emotions are too high to decide things like that."

"Would you consider going to work for Big Pharma?" asked Rick.

"I could. I have the credentials. I'm not sure. Maybe if they had a performance-enhancing division, just for the experience before I start my own company," replied Adam.

The sun began to set, so they headed to the restaurant. Jules had made a reservation for them, and they arrived a few minutes early but were seated right away. The restaurant was as good as Rick remembered. After dinner, they were all a little worn out from all the driving and headed back to the hotel in New Orleans.

Rick allowed Chief to stay with Adam and his mom in his room. She was as fascinated by Chief as Adam was, and Chief seemed to warm up to her nicely. Rick changed into some loose shorts and a tank top while Jules searched for something to watch on Netflix. She usually liked true crime, but after spending so much time in the courtroom lately, they settled on a comedy and picked *The Adam Project* with Ryan Reynolds, which was fitting since Adam in the next room was a project for Rick. As tired as they were, they managed to stay up for the entire movie because it was just that good. When the movie finished, out of the blue, Jules said,

"Rick, we need a honeymoon."

He cocked his head and replied,

"Why, yes, we do. Where would you like to go?"

"How about Italy? Renato lives there somewhere, so it'll be easy for him to come, and we can invite the gang for a celebration; we can stay on the Amalfi Coast first, rent a little villa on the water, and chill out."

"That sounds amazing, Jules!"

"We can snuggle the entire time like two pigs in a comforter."

"That's two pigs in a blanket, you mean," said Rick.

"No, that's a breakfast treat."

"Never mind. I love you," said Rick as he chuckled and kissed her on the forehead.

After the movie, they settled into bed. Before they did anything, Jules planned to get Rick to go to the gym with her and work off all that bad food they'd eaten.

"Good morning, sunshine. Are you ready to work out?" asked Jules.

"Can I have a cup of coffee first?"

She scratched her chin, pretending to deliberate.

"Well, just this once."

After Rick downed a few cups of coffee, he followed Jules to the gym. He knew she was going to kick his butt. She made him stretch, then warmed up on an elliptical machine for thirty minutes. Together, they completed the entire weightlifting circuit; she referred to the notes she had shared on the family plan with Rick on her iPhone, which he had taken from Adam, and they began the kettlebell routine. Rick moved up to a twenty-five-pound kettlebell, and it made a huge difference. He knew he was going to be sore as hell the next day.

"Can I please get a massage?" Rick asked.

"I already booked us a couples massage because I knew you'd be whining. Let's go, you big baby."

Rick pretended to suck his thumb as they made their way to the day spa. The massages were wonderful, and Rick drank a ton of water afterward. He wished he had some of that special recovery drink that Adam made from scratch. Since they didn't have anything to do he knocked on Adam's door and asked him if he could make some of the powder so Rick could have some for later.

"We'll need to find a lab nearby that sells the raw ingredients and get a few mixing bowls and other things, but it's boring and my mom is here," said Adam.

"Mrs. Olsen, do you like shopping?" asked Jules.

"What woman doesn't?" she replied.

"Why don't the boys go get the ingredients for Adam's recovery mix, and you and I can walk down to the shops at the French Market? We drove by it, remember?" asked Jules.

"Oh yeah, that cute little open-air place."

"Okay, it's settled. You two go play Mr. Olympia, and Mrs. Olsen and I will go spend some of your money, Rick," said Jules.

"Call me Freja," said Adam's mom.

"Okay, Freja it is."

"TDAL Partners is nearby, and they have everything I need, Rick. I'll bring my SciShield ID, which allows me to purchase chemicals and powders in bulk. Some items can be obtained from regular supply houses, but for the purest ingredients, we should go to the lab. I know we can get Creatine Monohydrate Powder, Betaine, L-Carnitine L-Tartrate, and a few more things I'll need, including my secret ingredient," said Adam.

"What's your secret ingredient?"

"It's a secret, duh! Just kidding. I have the recipe in my notes. I'll text it to you now. I trust you," said Adam.

Rick's phone vibrated with a text from Adam. He read that the entire recipe, including the secret ingredient, was somatropin, a special powdered form of HGH, aka human growth hormone. Rick stepped into his room, quickly changed clothes, then he and Adam took the elevator to the parking garage. When they arrived at the lab supply house, Adam showed the receptionist his ID, and Rick was allowed inside as long as he stayed with Adam. The lab supply house was also an active lab in addition to being a supply house. They passed several large windows where men in white coats worked with machines Rick had only seen on Forensic Files before. He had memorized one machine in particular that always caught his fancy.

"Look, Adam, there's a gas chromatography/mass spectrometer."

"Wow! I'm impressed. How'd you know that?" asked Adam.

"I'm smart. Nah, just kidding. I memorized it from a TV show I watch."

As they walked down the hall, a clerk walked by and lifted his head as he approached Adam.

"Hey, back again?"

Adam didn't respond and had a confused look on his face.

"You know him?" asked Rick.

"Nope, never been here before. I must look like someone he knows. Maybe I have a doppelgänger."

"We all do."

Once they had all the ingredients, beakers and measuring tools they needed, Adam got a case of plastic tubes with locking lids, so he could make up a bunch of the powder that Rick could pop open and pour into a bottle of water. They returned to the hotel and to be on the safe side, Rick put Chief in his hotel room and closed the adjoining door while Adam mixed the powders. It took him about an hour.

"Hand me one of those bottles of water from the mini fridge and take a little sip first," said Adam.

Rick did that and handed Adam the bottle. He measured out a dose of the powder, poured it into the bottle, and shook it up.

"Give it a try."

Rick took a sip and licked his lips.

"I taste pineapple."

"Yep, I remember you saying you liked that taste, so I put pure pineapple extract powder in this batch. That part is easy to change, so if Jules prefers something else like cherry or strawberry, it's easy to fix," said Adam.

"Should I drink the whole bottle now?"

"Yeah. Go ahead."

Rick downed the bottle, and he wasn't sure if it was in his head or real, but he felt energized and less fatigued since his workout. Jules and Mrs. Olsen returned with arms full of shopping bags an hour later, and Rick mixed up one for Jules to try.

"Wow, that's good."

"Yep, Adam says he can do any flavor for us. Look in the closet," said Rick.

Jules stepped into their room and opened the closet door. Sitting on the little dresser inside was a case of red plastic tubes with locking flip caps. They looked just like the tubes she'd seen in Costco for Zipfizz.

"Wow, that's awesome. You made all these, Adam?" she asked with a raised voice.

He hollered back, "Yes."

Jules showed Rick all the things she had bought at the French Market and told him Mrs. Olsen thoroughly enjoyed herself.

"She did express concern and fear over the proceedings tomorrow," said Jules.

"It's understandable. He's an only child. In her mind, Adam is still her little boy."

"Yeah, I get that. Do you think it will go his way?" asked Jules.

"I can't say with a hundred percent guarantee, but if I were a betting man, and I am, I think Adam will walk out of that courtroom a free man tomorrow."

Adam and his mother visited next door, and when it was close to dinnertime, Rick knocked on the adjoining door.

"Would you two like to eat dinner with us downstairs, or would you prefer to eat in your room?" asked Rick.

"I think I'd like to spend as much time with my mom as possible in case things don't go my way. I hope I'm not being rude," said Adam.

"Not at all Adam. I understand completely. Order whatever you would like and we will see you in the morning."

Rick and Jules took the elevator down to the restaurant in the hotel. Even though it was dinnertime, neither of them had much of an appetite. The reality of the case lingered with them. Although things looked extremely good for Adam, if they were wrong, there was always a chance he could be found guilty and sentenced to death. They both ordered salads and went to bed early. Anxiety had crept into them both. They had grown fond of Adam, especially after seeing him with his mom. Deep down, they felt he couldn't have committed such a heinous crime.

They both woke up before their alarms went off. As they got dressed for court, it felt as if they were preparing for a funeral. Rick switched from his black suit to a blue one because of that thought. He even pulled out his lucky rabbit's foot and put it in his right trouser pocket. They all drove together to the courthouse in relative silence. When they parked, Rick turned to Adam and squeezed his arm.

"Everything is gonna be alright."

They entered the courtroom, which was packed to capacity with people filling the hallways and reporters and cameras everywhere. Adam joined Todd at the defense table as they waited for the judge to enter the courtroom. Rick was on pins and needles, and his hands were shaking. He wished he had taken a Xanax before he came. Jules held his hand, then grabbed Possum's. Gary sat on the inside and patted Possum on the hand.

The judge opened the door behind the bench and made his way toward his seat.

"All rise," said the bailiff.

"Be seated," said the judge as he sat down.

"Your Honor, may I approach the bench?" asked the prosecutor, David Reed.

Both the prosecutor and the defense approached the bench. The prosecutor spoke quietly to the judge. Both counselors were nodding, and the judge appeared frustrated. After a few minutes, both lawyers returned to their tables.

"Ladies and gentlemen, there has been a new development in the trial. You may proceed, Mr. Reed."

"Thank you, Your Honor. Upon reviewing newly introduced evidence to the state, the people would like to dismiss all charges with prejudice against the defendant, Mr. Adam Olsen."

The crowd erupted, and the judge pounded his gavel several times.

"Quiet in the courtroom," said the judge.

Nearly everyone in the courtroom sat on the edge of their seat, holding their breath as they waited for the judge to finish speaking.

"Let the record reflect the State has moved to dismiss all charges against the defendant with prejudice. This court understands that to mean the case is permanently closed—these charges may not be brought again, in this courtroom or any other," said the judge as he adjusted his glasses.

"Is there any objection from the defense?"

"No, Your Honor."

The judge nodded.

"Very well. The motion is granted. All charges are hereby dismissed with prejudice.

Mr. Olsen, you are free to go. This case is concluded. The court is adjourned," said Judge Morgan.

The judge's gavel fell for the last time. The crowd erupted in cheers once again. Adam broke down, reached over, and hugged Todd. Tears streamed down Jules' face as she squeezed Rick's hand. Rick welled up and pulled Jules close, burying his head in her hair to hide his tears. They all rushed to the defense table and embraced Todd and Adam together. Adam's legs felt weak, and he nearly collapsed from all the emotion.

"You ready to get the hell out of here?" asked Rick to Adam.

"Let's go. We need to address the press," added Todd.

The group pushed their way into the courtroom hallway as camera flashes popped and microphones were thrust forward. Reporters clustered around them as they walked, yelling questions. Outside, in front of the entrance, was a podium set up with dozens of microphones. Todd stepped up with Adam beside him and cleared his throat.

"Good morning. As you're all aware, the State has formally moved to dismiss all charges in the case of State vs. Olsen, with prejudice. That means this matter is closed. Permanently. My client cannot be tried for this murder again under any circumstances. Today, he is a free man. We thank the court for its time, and we respect the process. That will be our final comment on the matter."

"Adam, do you have anything to say?" asked one reporter near the podium.

Todd looked over to Adam to see if he wanted to speak. He nodded.

"I just want to thank my entire defense team, as well as private detective Mr. Rick Waters and his entire group. They believed in me from the beginning, and I am forever grateful," said Adam.

They all hurried away from the courthouse steps to the parking garage. Rick, Jules, Adam, and his mom made their way to the hotel in relative silence. Adam's mom grasped his arm, her face beaming with joy. Upon reaching the hotel, they all let out a sigh of relief.

"It's over," said Rick, proclaiming out loud what everyone was thinkin

CHAPTER
EIGHTEEN

Possum and Gary arrived at the hotel, walking in with Todd and Anthony. Gary was carrying a six pack of Busch tallboys and a bottle of champagne.

"Woohoo! Time to celebrate!" exclaimed Gary.

Gary and Possum hugged Adam. Possum popped open the champagne, startling Chief. He took a big swig and handed it to Adam, who took a huge sip and poured some over his head as if he had just won the Daytona 500. He passed the bottle to Gary who chugged the remainder. Rick's room was at capacity.

"Let's take this celebration to the club lounge," said Rick.

"Good idea," replied Gary.

The rooms they were staying in were on the club level and featured a fully stocked club lounge with snacks, beer, wine, and mixed drinks, as well as a concierge and bartender. They celebrated exuberantly. Gary wanted to plan a big dinner for the night and asked Jules to find the best restaurant in New Orleans. After they calmed down a bit and the emotions settled, Adam pulled Gary aside to talk to him privately.

"Gary, I don't know how to thank you. I have no idea how much you had to pay Todd to defend me, and I don't know how I'm going to pay you back, but I promise I will," said Adam.

"I have an idea. Rick shared the proprietary recipe of your recovery drink mix that you texted him. He told you that you were looking for an investor to start a health supplement line. Instead of an investor, how would you like a partner? That recovery mix can be the first flagship product of the line," said Gary.

Adam's eyes widened and he stuck out his hand for Gary to shake.

"Let's do it!" said Adam.

They shook hands to seal the deal between Gary and Adam with a gentleman's agreement. Gary didn't disclose how much he paid Todd and his team to represent him, nor did he mention the hotel room, flights for his mom, or meals; but it was over seven hundred fifty thousand dollars. For him, it was worth it. How could one put a price on another innocent man's freedom?

Jules chose Desi Vega's Steakhouse for dinner. Besides being one of the highest-rated restaurants in New Orleans, they also offered a private dining special menu complete with a mashed potato bar, iced seafood display, deluxe char-cuterie board, and chef's carving station. The carving station featured USDA Prime filet mignon tenderloin, freshly roasted turkey breast, and herb-coated cedar plank salmon. For an additional fee, they could have a private bartender with an open bar and a premium dessert table. There was no doubt that Gary would want the deluxe package, which also included every conceivable side dish and two private waiters.

They all went to their separate rooms to wind down and relax. Adam's mom needed to get back to Denmark because one of her nieces was in the hospital to have a baby, and she wanted to be there. Gary arranged for a car to the airport and first-class tickets for her. They all said goodbye to her, and Adam rode with her to ensure she was checked in and on the flight.

Rick told Jules he felt like working out and was surprised that he wasn't as sore as he thought he would be. The recovery mix that Adam had created worked wonders. Rick grabbed two tubes of it from the closet along with two bottles of water and shook them up. He and Jules headed down to the gym, where he placed them in a small mini fridge in the corner. After an intense workout, they opted for couples massages again. They both drank their recovery drinks and proceeded to the day spa.

They showered and put on robes to relax the rest of the day until the dinner party.

"I'm so happy," said Jules.

"Yeah, me too, baby. It feels good to know that Adam is a free man. We may never figure out who killed Paul, although I suspect it was Jason Bagley. But since Jason was killed, I guess karma caught up with him, or someone got to him and that Bill or whatever his name is, and this goes deeper than we know. It almost feels like a mob hit; a murder conspiracy to keep them quiet, or they might have accidentally seen something the night Paul was murdered and were loose ends. Adam was just an easy target. I think I'm going to investigate further. I'm beginning to think that Paul might have owed the wrong people some money, and whoever killed him framed Adam since he was the significant other," Rick explained.

"That last theory makes the most sense," said Jules.

"There is a local mafia here called the Cajun Connection. I do remember Paul saying he went to Harrah's Casino often. Maybe he took out a marker that he couldn't pay back. I bet the mob has their fingers in that casino."

"Maybe we should just walk away. Adam is free and the last thing we want is the mob putting a hit on us for snooping around," said Jules.

"You may be right. Maybe after we finish the movie, we should think about getting out of town. Ever since you said we should do our honeymoon on the Amalfi Coast, it's all I can think about."

"Oh, Rick, that would be so wonderful," said Jules.

Gary hired a van to take everyone to the restaurant. He brought a little cooler with him full of Busch Light tallboys.

"You can't bring those into the restaurant, Gary," said Rick.

"The hell I can't. You've heard of a corking fee for wine, right? Well, for what I'm paying for this dinner, they better offer me a corking fee for these beers!"

Rick just shook his head. You could take Gary out of redneck country, but you couldn't take the country redneck out of him. When they arrived, they were greeted by the owner, who summoned a hostess to escort them to the private room. He followed them in.

"Anything y'all need. I do mean anything, do not hesitate to ask," said the owner.

Gary opened the little cooler filled with Busch Light beers, and without hesitation, he had the bartender in the private room put them on ice for him. They all sat down at a massive round table. The hostess closed the double doors to the private room, and the liquor started flowing. Gary was an odd duck. He'd drink just about anything as long as he had Busch Lights to go with it. He had the restaurant order some Dom Perignon and non-alcoholic Giesen New Zealand Sparkling Brut for Rick and Jules. He also ordered some Guinness 0 for Rick and some Athletic Free Wave Hazy IPA for Jules.

The waiter poured everyone either a glass of champagne or brut as Gary stood up to make a toast. Rick had also prepared a little toast and planned to speak after Gary. Gary's was off the cuff, but Rick would read his from his iPhone notes.

"To Adam. We are all so thrilled that you are a free man. It cost me a pretty penny, but it was worth it. Now that we are done with that stinking trial, let's make some money together. I think we could do a bunch of different flavors of your recovery drink mix. We could do one with apple flavor and call it Adam's Apple. Get it? Adam's Apple?" asked Gary.

"Wait, wait, before you down it all, I have written a little poem. Jules brought my guitar from the motorhome to the hotel, and I was fooling around with it earlier, but it's too raw, so I'll just read it."

Rick cleared his throat and began.

Poor Adam was minding his business one day,
When cops kicked the door in and dragged him away.
"Murder!" they cried, "It had to be you!"
He said, "Wait—me?! Is it just cuz I'm gay?!"

"Sorry, Adam, it rhymed," said Rick.

Adam laughed and said, "Just continue."

They cuffed him, they stuffed him, they read him his rights,
He missed Taco Tuesday and Netflix that night.
The headlines all read, "Real Zombie On Set!"
He was the only one they had in their sights.

"Boo," yelled everyone. The boos weren't directed at the poem but at the cops who never considered any other suspects except Adam.

"Okay, last line and I'm done," said Rick.

The smug prosecutor thought he would win
He proclaimed loudly, "He's guilty as sin!"
But the video proved that it was misconstrued
And the case was dismissed, in the end.

Everyone applauded, hooted, and hollered, and Rick got a standing ovation. Adam came over and hugged him.

"That was great, Rick!" he said.

"Let's eat!" exclaimed Gary.

The waiters introduced a fried Caesar salad, consisting of a flash-fried cone of parmesan cheese filled with a rich Caesar salad. It looked like a salad ice cream cone lying on its side. They also offered cheese planks, which were similar to cheese sticks but made with exceptionally rich imported Italian mozzarella. Rick absolutely loved cheese sticks, and these were the best he'd ever tasted. They all took turns selecting fresh seafood from the iced seafood display tray, which was loaded with chilled jumbo shrimp, marinated crab claws, oysters on the half shell, ahi tuna poke cups, and Maine lobster medallions. As good as that was the chef's carving station was spectacular.

Rick took a bit of each: filet, salmon, and turkey breast. Jules got a nice cut of filet mignon and salmon. Gary did the same and went back for seconds; so did Possum. Everyone loved the meal and got their fill. Just when they thought it was over, a waiter rolled out a massive dessert tray covered with an assortment of petit fours, brownies, jelly rolls, strawberry or chocolate Russian cake, apricot squares, Champagne patties, white or chocolate almond squares, assorted doberge squares, rum balls, buttercream bites, cheesecake bites with assorted sauces, and mini red velvet brownies with cream cheese frosting. It was like nothing they'd ever seen before.

After dessert, they stayed late and had after-dinner drinks. No one wanted the party to end, and the owner kept the staff late after the main part of the restaurant had closed. Gary paid the bill and personally tipped each of the staff several hundred dollars. The entire staff was ecstatic. The driver pulled the van out front, and Possum helped Gary stumble and get in. He had a huge buzz. Rick and Possum helped Gary into his room and made sure he was in bed and comfortable. Rick made him a recovery drink in a water bottle and forced him to drink it. Rick knew it would make him feel better when he woke up in the morning. He put another mixed-up water bottle in Gary's mini fridge. Rick returned to his room, got undressed, and climbed into bed with Jules. He fell asleep beside her, snuggled up tight.

Rick woke up feeling great. He was glad he didn't drink anymore. Since Possum knew the party would go late, he gave the cast, crew, and extras one more day off from filming. Rick wanted to take it easy and relax in the hotel. He contemplated whether to go to the pool, the day spa, or just chill in the room. But first things first, he needed coffee. He brewed a fresh pot as Jules slept in. He poured a cup and picked up his guitar in the living room, starting to play a few chords quietly.

Jules had surprised him a while back with a carbon fiber McPherson guitar. It was perfect for the motorhome because it didn't contain any wood, so when the motorhome was in storage, he could leave it inside without fear of it warping. He loved the way it sounded when plugged into a small guitar amp or PA system, but he wasn't sure how it sounded unplugged. He pulled out the sound hole cover, which was designed to block feedback, but unfortunately muted the sound when it was unplugged. Since Jules couldn't play chords, the only way for him to know how it sounded unplugged was to record it and listen back. He remembered reading about a good app for iPhones for recording and searched for it in the App Store. It was great because it recorded at a high-quality frequency of 96 kHz/24 bit and saved space because it only recorded when sound was audible. He could hit record, leave it on and walk away, then return, pick up his guitar and strum again and it would record once more.

He couldn't remember the name of the app, but after searching for a while, he found it. It was called Spire: Music Recorder and Studio. After he downloaded it, he was surprised to find out that he could record individual tracks as well and mix them like in a studio.

"I'm gonna jump in the shower. Can you order some bagels or something?" shouted Jules from the bedroom.

"Okay, baby. As soon as I finish this download."

Rick installed the app on his iPhone, picked up his guitar, and hit record. He played a few chords, stopped, and listened to it. It sounded great. Instead of ordering from the hotel, he thought he'd surprise Jules by having some Humble Bagels delivered via Uber Eats. He hit record again and played a few chords, pausing as he stopped, just like he had read. He set down the guitar and walked over to the adjoining door to see if Adam wanted bagels too. He turned around and grabbed his iPhone so he could order whatever Adam wanted, then knocked on the door. No one answered, so Rick popped his head in and didn't see anyone.

The bed looked like Adam had just climbed out of it, so Rick figured he was in the bathroom. He was about to back into his room and wait when he saw something on Adam's nightstand that took his breath away. In a short glass of water lay a single denture. Just as Rick spotted it, Adam stepped out of the bathroom. He looked up at Rick, staring at the partial denture, and slowly gave Rick an evil smile, revealing the gap in his teeth. Rick just stood there for a second, motionless and speechless. He was taken aback and stunned.

"It was you, wasn't it?" asked Rick. "You killed Paul."

There was a moment of silence in the room as they sized each other up.

"Did you also kill Jason and Bill, I mean Friedrich? How? Why? I don't get it. I saw you on the video. I saw the guy spike your drink with GHB. Plus, your Under Armor personalized insulated cup was under the wood plank in Jason's kitchen. You have the ability to get thallium with your SciShield ID. You poisoned them."

"Elementary, my dear Watson. I thought you figured it out when we went to the lab and that guy recognized me in the hall. That's where I got the thallium from. He works on the other side of the building in the NIOSH center where they keep the. highly toxic stuff. I never thought I'd run into him where they supply the health supplements bulk powders. I may as well tell you everything. My case was dismissed. I can't be tried again for Paul's murder, and good luck proving I killed Jason and Friedrich," said Adam.

"So, you did kill them. Why?"

"It's quite simple really. I discovered that Paul was sleeping with Jason, and I hate cheaters. Paul had to pay, so I killed him and his lover Jason."

"What about Friedrich?" asked Rick.

"Collateral damage, I'm afraid. He was just in the wrong place at the wrong time. I was stuffing Paul's body in the freezer, and he walked in and saw me. Just bad luck," said Adam.

"But I saw a man with a limp in a tracksuit spike your Under Armor cap with GHB and then plant the murder weapon and duffel bag in the dumpster!"

Adam fake limped over to the closet and pulled out a black tracksuit.

"You mean a black tracksuit like this?"

"But I saw two people on the camera. Wait..." Rick said as he thought back. "I never saw two people on that surveillance video at the same time."

"Exactly. You saw what I wanted you to see. After I finished my bench press, I stepped through the door of the locker room, quickly threw on my tracksuit and glasses, then made my way from the locker room to the pool and back into the gym through the door from the pool. I hovered over the treadmill and glanced back toward the locker room as if someone had cracked it open. I stepped off, put the GHB in my cup, then walked back through the pool door into the locker room, took off the tracksuit, and changed back into my shorts and tank top. After taking a big swig from my cup, I did my kettlebell exercises. I slipped back into the locker room, hid the tracksuit and cup in the ceiling panel, and then walked into view of the pool camera, where I eventually succumbed to the GHB. It was perfect timing. I had taken GHB recreationally many times and knew exactly how much I needed to pass out and how long it would take to hit me," said Adam.

"But how'd you get the cup to Jason's house and plant it under the loose plank in the kitchen? You said you hid it in the ceiling in the locker room, and you were with me ever since they found you and you were released from jail," said Rick.

"I have to give you credit for that, Rick. Finding that cup at Jason's was some good detective work. Do you really think there could be only one Under Armor insulated cup in the world? Paul had two of them made for me. One for when we travel and one I leave in Germany. But I actually brought them both by accident when we returned to Germany from Egypt. That's when I found messages on Paul's phone from Jason and I started planning the murder. Jason had been visiting Germany to see Paul for a while behind my back. They met at Oktoberfest. I usually go to that but I was sick and missed one. That fucker Paul has been cheating on me for quite a while. Fuck him! He's dead now."

"I have to hand it to you Adam. I'm impressed. You framed yourself to prove you didn't do it. I never saw that coming," said Rick.

"I know it's a lot to take in. Listen we can keep this between us. I still want to work with Gary. Paul and Jason deserved it. I feel bad about Friedrich, but shit happens. Please think about it. You can't turn me in. No one would believe that crazy story anyway, and it's not like I'm going to confess to the cops. Just think about it at least."

Rick nodded.

"You're right; you basically have double jeopardy with Paul, and without a confession, there's no way to prove the other two murders. I'll think about it. I need some time to register all this. I sort of understand why you did it. I might have done the same thing," lied Rick. "There's no need for it to go any further than this room. We can keep it between us, and I certainly won't tell Jules or Gary. She's grown quite fond of you, and Gary has big plans to go into business with you and your recovery drink mix. When it comes to making money, Gary can overlook a few transgressions. He's no angel himself."

"I'm glad you see it my way, Rick. Thank you," said Adam.

Rick nodded and stepped back through the adjoining door into his hotel room, closing and locking it behind him. He glanced at his iPhone and saw that ten minutes of audio had been recorded. He stepped into the bathroom, rewound the recording, then cupped his hand over the phone to muffle the volume and listened. It had captured Paul's entire confession. Rick hit save on the recording app, backed it up to the cloud, forwarded it to Carson, and then texted him that he'd call him in five minutes. He put his finger to his lips to signal Jules to be quiet, then motioned for her to follow him to the lobby. The silent security alarm was still on Adam's door. He carefully opened the door to the hallway, and they slipped out of the room. When they got to the lobby, Rick spilled the beans.

"We have a problem. Listen to this," said Rick.

Jules listened in disbelief to the entire confession from Adam that Rick had secretly recorded. Her eyes told the story. As she listened, they changed from disbelief to betrayal and finally to anger and fear.

"What are we going to do?" asked Jules.

"I need you to go to the sheriff's department and find the lead investigator. You will be safe there. I'm going to airdrop this to your phone I already forwarded a copy to Carson.

Adam killed three people, which qualifies him as a serial killer. I bet he's killed in the past as well, back in Europe. When he confessed to me, his eyes were cold, and he said he was sorry, but it didn't feel real. It felt rehearsed. We have to get him into custody before he hurts someone else. He has no idea I feel this way. I convinced him that I understand and would probably do the same thing under the circumstances. He's too dangerous for you to be around, so take my keys and go now."

Jules headed for the parking garage and Rick called Carson.

"Carson, did you listen?" asked Rick.

"Yeah, as a former FBI profiler, I can tell you that guy is a psychopath and a serial killer. Where is he now?"

"He's in the room adjoining mine. I'm down in the lobby. I have convinced him that I am empathetic to why he did it. He has no clue I'm calling you. I sent Jules to the sheriff's department to keep her safe and share the recording with the lead detective. We need to get him into custody, so I need your help. Can you call in the cavalry?" asked Rick.

"I already did. I sent it to a friend over at the Louisiana State Police. They are putting together a SWAT unit now. That recording is enough to secure an arrest warrant and take him in. You just need to keep him there. Can you do that?"

"Oh yeah. Jules is safe so that it won't be a problem. I'll head back up and make sure he doesn't go anywhere. How soon can SWAT get here?" asked Rick.

"Within the hour," responded Carson.

Rick texted Gary to ask him where he was.

I'm at the gym. Woke up feeling great after drinking one of Adam's recover drinks.

Come to lobby, immediately.

10-4, on my way.

Gary got down to the lobby within two minutes.

"What's so urgent?" asked Gary.

Rick played the recording for Gary. He frowned as he listened.

"That son of a bitch played us. He has to go down for this. I had big plans to start a business with him. What a waste," said Gary.

"You still can start the business," said Rick with a grin as he showed Gary the recipe with the secret ingredient for Adam's recovery drink.

"You got the formula!" exclaimed Gary, "Now what do we do?"

"Are you ready to put on your actor's hat? Let's go to Adam's room. SWAT will be here within the hour to take him down. We just need to keep him here. Let's go pitch a business plan to Adam to keep him busy until SWAT gets here."

"Good plan. Can you somehow get SWAT to knock on the door instead of kicking it down? I can make up a story that I'm having the contract delivered by my attorney this morning to his room," said Gary

"I love it. Let's do this."

Rick texted Carson the plan and received a thumbs-up in response. Rick and Gary headed to Adam's room. Rick knocked, and they stepped inside. Rick's silent alarm on his phone vibrated when the door opened, confirming it was still activated.

"Adam, I have to tell you, I am blown away by your recovery drink. I drank way too much liquor last night, but I had one of your formulas before going to bed and another when I woke up, and I have no hangover. I felt so good that I actually wanted to work out, so I went to the gym this morning," said Gary with excitement.

"Really? That's great," responded Adam.

"It got me thinking. We can actually have two businesses together using the same product. We can market it under different names. One can be a recovery drink for post-workouts, and the other can be marketed as a hangover cure. That stuff can be sold at every liquor store in the country by the register on an impulse display rack. We can sell them as single units for a huge markup and sell them in a thirty-pack box at GNC and other health stores as a sports recovery mix. I bet I can even get it into Walmart and Costco. I have my lawyer coming over with the contracts. He's on his way. I thought we could brainstorm a name for the hangover cure while we wait for the contracts to arrive. You'll need to have your own lawyer look them over, but I assure you, you will be pleased with the arrangement."

"Wow, Gary, what a great idea. I'm so happy we are going to be partners. I can't wait to get the contracts," said Adam.

Gary was delivering a masterclass on business pitches in Adam's room, and he was buying it hook, line, and sinker. They brainstormed names for the hangover cure mix, and after half an hour, there was a knock on the door.

"That must be my lawyer," said Gary.

"I'll get it," said Adam as he jogged up to the door and opened it quickly,

The SWAT team bum rushed him and tackled him to the floor. They flipped him on his stomach and zip-tied his hands with flex cuffs. The lead detective walked in after Adam was secured.

"Mr. Adam Olsen, you are under arrest for the murder of Friedrich Wagner, and Jason Bagley You have the right to remain silent. Anything you say can be used against you in a court of law. You have the right to an attorney. If you cannot afford an attorney, one will be appointed for you, prior to and during any questioning, if you wish. Do you understand your rights?" asked the detective.

Adam nodded.

"I need a verbal answer," replied the detective.

"Yes," said Adam as they lifted him to his feet.

He looked at Rick and Gary with a hatred that Rick had never encountered before. Adam's eyes were cold and dark—like the deranged, evil eyes of a serial killer. They led him out of the room. Jules walked in a few moments later and joined Rick and Gary.

"Now what?" asked Gary.

I guess now you're starting your new business with Adam's proprietary formula, and Jules and I are going on our honeymoon once we finish this zombie film, of course.

"Where are y'all gonna go?" asked Gary.

"Italy: the Amalfi Coast first for a week, then we'd like all y'all to fly out, and we'll throw a big shindig and invite Renato," replied Rick.

"A party! I'll bring the hangover cure!" exclaimed Gary.

THE END

ACKNOWLEDGMENTS

I want to thank my beta readers, Mike Keevil and Chris Bowers.

I want to thank my amazing editors, Arly Gramm and Izzy Lily.

I want to thank my proofreader, Teri Rogers.

Thanks to my graphic artist Les.

Special thanks to Nick Sullivan, Wayne Stinnett and Bob Adamov for all their support and advice over the years.

I want to thank all the readers of my novels especially. It's all about the readers. I appreciate your continued support on this journey.

ABOUT THE AUTHOR

Eric Chance Stone was born and raised on the Gulf Coast of Southeast Texas. An avid surfer, sailor, scuba diver, fisherman, and treasure hunter, Eric met many bigger-than-life characters on his global adventures. Wanting to travel after college, he got a job with Northwest Airlines and moved to Florida. Shortly after that, he was transferred to Hawaii, then Nashville. After years of being a staff songwriter in Nashville, he released his first album, Songs For Sail, in 1999, a tropically inspired collection of songs. He continued to write songs and tour and eventually landed a gig with Sail America and Show Management to perform at all international boat shows, where his list of characters continued to grow.

He moved to the Virgin Islands in 2007 and became the official entertainer for Pusser's Marina Cay in the BVI. After several years in the Caribbean, his fate for telling stories was sealed.

Upon releasing his 15th CD, All The Rest, he was inspired to become a novelist after meeting with Wayne Stinnett. Wayne, along with Cap Daniels, Chip Bell, and a few others, became his mentors, and they are all good friends now. Eric resides in a 44' Entegra Aspire motorhome with his fiancée Kim-Cara. They live wherever they are parked.

Inspired by the likes of Clive Cussler's Dirk Pitt, Wayne Stinnett's Jesse McDermitt, Cap Daniels Chase Fulton, Chip Bell's Jake Sullivan, and many more, Eric's tales are sprinkled with Voodoo, Hoodoo, and kinds of weird stuff. From the bayous of Texas to the Voodoo dens of Haiti, his twist of reality will take you for a ride. His main character, Rick Waters, is a down-to-earth good ol' boy and adventurist turned private eye who uses his treasure-hunting skills and street smarts to solve mysteries.

ALSO BY ERIC CHANCE STONE

Blue Waters

Vanishing Waters

Raging Waters

Back Waters

Muddy Waters

Mayan Waters

African Waters

Deep Waters

Baja Waters

Canuck Waters

Junkanoo Waters

Arctic Waters

Pirate Waters

Dark Waters

Persian Waters

Rising Waters - Coming Soon

www.ingramcontent.com/pod-product-compliance
Lightning Source LLC
Chambersburg PA
CBHW060909250626
47159CB00008B/2924